SINATRALAND

SINATRALAND

SAM KASHNER

THE OVERLOOK PRESS
WOODSTOCK & NEW YORK

Thanks to Tracy Carns, Albert DePetrillo and to
Peter Mayer for their help and many kindnesses.

First published in the United States in 1999 by
The Overlook Press, Peter Mayer Publishers, Inc.
Lewis Hollow Road
Woodstock, New York 12498

Library of Congress Cataloging-in-Publication Data

Kashner, Sam.
Sinatraland / Sam Kashner.
p.   cm.
I. Title.
PS3561.A697S56   1999   813'.54—dc21   98-47734

Book design by Chris Morran and Bernard Schleifer
Manufactured in the United States of America
First Edition
1 3 5 7 9 8 6 4 2

CONTENTS

Love and Marriage
9

Glad to Be Unhappy
61

Strangers in the Night
105

The Second Time Around
155

Everything Happens to Me
177

*For my sister, Gella Pearl
and for Nick Parash, Leslie Daniels &
Nancy, of course. In gratitude.*

LOVE AND MARRIAGE

"Strange to be one's *name* no longer."

—JOHN BERRYMAN
From "Sonnets to Chris"

Dear Frank,

I bet you never thought you'd hear from your old pal Finkie. That's right, Francis. It's me. I've been trying to think of what to say to you after all this time, ever since I heard you were laid up in the hospital with gall bladder troubles. Alas, the Hoboken Finkelsteins are no more. Scattered to the four winds. And my brother Morris, "the creep" I think you used to call him, is dead. Not really dead, but my parents—you remember Miriam and Seymour Finkelstein?—they don't refer to Morris anymore ever since he ran off with a shiksa named Roberta. Can you believe it, Frank? I mean Morris still had strap lines on his arm from the tfillin. I'm sure you've heard of it, Frank. It's like in *The Man with the Golden Arm*, remember, when you tied a belt or was it a tie around your arm? Well, the Jews do it on both arms and keep a little leather box on their forehead when they pray. Otto Preminger is a Jew. Did you know that, Frank? Personally, I think it's disgusting his playing a Nazi like that. But what can you do? That's show business, am I right, Francis, or am I right?

Speaking of show business, our paths did cross one night in 1958. You would have considered it a close call. But I thought

I'd tell you what exactly transpired so you wouldn't get the wrong idea or hear it from some other unreliable source and misconstrue my drift.

It was 1958 like I just said and you were sitting in a booth at the Imperial Gardens having dinner with who else but Lauren Bacall. I know, Frank, how good you were to Betty (if I may call her that) after Bogie's untimely demise from lung cancer. How as Bogie's pal you didn't want Betty to mourn in loneliness. Well, anyhoo, you were sitting at the Imperial Gardens, Mrs. Bogart in attendance like I said and who do you think should be in the neighborhood but yours truly? I was on a business trip for the window shade company Weiss & Rifkind which I represent, and there was a trade show that week in the Cow Palace, and so I decided to drive up the coast to movieland and take in the sights. Well, it just so happens that an old pal of mine—we sold peanuts together one summer at the Polo Grounds—his firm had done some work for the owner of the Imperial Gardens, and as a favor to this fellow, the owner gave him free dinners for himself and a guest. But when Sy came for me at my hotel, Frank, I was sick as a dog perhaps due to the change in the water or what have you so I just begged off. But imagine my surprise when the next day I read in Louella's column that she had actually been at the Imperial Gardens having dinner when she overheard you proposing to Betty and I figured out it must've been just over a year since Bogie's death. You are one fast worker, Francis. I think, Frank, you are a lot like me. We both have romantic bents. Once at a party at my sister-in-law's house—just a private get together she threw before leaving for the Fountainbleu in Miami—I actually got up to sing and dedicated the number to the woman who would become my future ex-girlfriend.

I guess things didn't work out for you and Betty. I figured as much when I heard she'd gone to a Dean Martin opening at the Cocoanut Grove and she chose not to attend your triumphant opening at the Sands. There's a story there too but that'll have to wait. This is a lot of heavy lifting for a guy who just got out of the hospital. So I'll call a halt to things for a while. Although, you might be interested to know that I just purchased the largest home in Fort Lee. The real estate agent told me it briefly belonged to Buddy Hackett. Just thought you might want to know. Give 'em hell, Francis, and say hello to those cute little nurses for me.

Glad to be back in touch with

a pal,

Finkie

Dear Frank,

I'm glad you liked the flowers despite your allergies. How's a pal to know a thing like that? But when I heard you were laid up I got a terrible case of the guilt germs. I knew I had to help out someway. That's when I offered to send up some of Weiss & Rifkind's room darkeners. Frank, they're stupendous shades and are becoming a huge seller for us. I thought it would do a helluva job keeping the sunlight out of your room. So you wouldn't have to think about what you might be missing on the outside.

I even went over to Jilly's on 58th St. to ask Milton, the maitre d', about your condition. (Those gallstones must be worth a fortune, no?) I sat at the bar and waited. Frank, the place looks like a shrine. Our Lady of the perpetual party, according to Jilly. But I think you're working too hard, Francis, I can't keep up with you. *Some Came Running, Kings Go Forth, A Hole in the Head.* You've got to pace yourself. You can't be in two places with one tuchus, my grandmother used to say. So anyhoo, back to Jilly's. I'm sitting at the bar waiting for Mr. Rizzo to walk in. I'm certain Jilly's going to remember the nude body reading we used to do together. Did he ever tell you about that, Frank?

Whenever we'd meet a Miss America but couldn't decide how to divide the spoils, we'd just have some fun with the lovely lady instead of falling out over a dish. I would introduce Jilly as a world renowned body reader, someone who could tell a dish's future just from "reading" the shape of her curves. Like that thing they used to do a hundred years ago with the bumps in the head. Only this is on a doll's shape. Frank, you wouldn't believe how successful this was for yours truly and your faithful companion Mr. Rizzo. Once, on the 20th Century Limited, going to Chicago, we "body read" no fewer than nine babes in arms. There they would stand in our compartment on the train, swaying a little back and forth as the train headed for Chi—nothing shy about these babies, as me or Jilly read their future.

The only time I really felt like a heel, Frank, was when Jilly told this one chickadee that she was going to have six kids and marry a polo player named Rubirosa. It turns out that the future Mrs. Rubi had a scar running up her entire back. A wicked looking scar that you could've stuck your thumb into. Her future didn't look too good to me, Frank, I'll tell you that.

Needless to say, Jilly never showed up at Jilly's. So I ordered the leg of lamb and devoured it at the bar. A very delectable little fly sat down next to me and the next thing I know we're talking about you, Frank.

She saw you at Chez Paree in Chicago. So we compared notes. Seems like she can't decide if she likes you or Glenn Ford better in the movies. I offered to show her some of your other haunts in the city. Maybe Danny's Hideaway would have a booth with our name on it, open and waiting. But I didn't want to risk being told to wait for a table with a skirt in tow. So I got her work number and beat a hasty retreat. On the way home the cabbie was listening to the Pelvis. The entire trip back to the apartment, Francis, can you believe it? I agree with you, Frank, 110 percent about that hillbilly. Didn't you call rock-n-roll "the most vicious form of expression it has been my displeasure to hear"? I can't blame you, Frank, he's nothing but a hillbilly. He's an embarrassment to show business. Could you imagine him at Sy Devore's trying on a suit? The three way mirrors would look the other way. I saw where Perry Como, speaking of pretenders to the throne, is ranked 22nd on the all-time sales list and you, mine General, are 34th. Como's a cadaver. He should be disqualified on account of his not having a pulse. You will always be the pope, the general, el dago to me, pal.

Yours until Elvis Pretzel scuffs his blue suede shoes.

The Fink

Dear Frank,

I'm thinking a lot about Tami Mauriello and about how quickly a guy forgets. I remember when you had an interest in Tami. Ten thousand smackers I think it was. I sent a hundred bucks care of the Gotham Health Club to buy a piece of Tami myself. For a hundred bucks I guess I must've owned one of Tami's armpits or at least a couple of eyelashes. Someone at the Gotham once told me that you used to go there even after Tami got drafted and that you wore one of Tami's dogtags around your neck like a crucifix. You were the only guy I know who could kid Rocky Marciano or even Dempsey about their voices—high-pitched like a couple of schoolgirls. You'd tease them. You'd tell them they must've been hit in the crotch too many times. But all that aside, Frank, tonight I'm a little blue thinking about Tami Mauriello. I remember when Tami fought in the Garden (I think you even skipped out on a concert date to be there for him) but it didn't help Tami much. When he got out of the Army he seemed like a different kid. He always seemed to be thumbing worry beads in his head. I know he was the best bodyguard you could have. But somehow I thought Tami wanted something else out of life other than keeping little teenage girls from crowding you. I once offered Tami a job with Weiss & Rifkind. I offered to show him the ropes, thought he'd make a helluva good salesman. "Wow, you're Tami Mauriello. I saw you fight in the crusades, back in the old Polo Ground days. I'll take 1500 scalloped fringe shades from now till the Messiah comes!" But then the roof caved in on Weiss & Rifkind and we were all SOL (shit out of luck). Well that's the thing about the shade business Frank, it has its ups and downs. (I thought I would try to cheer us both up with a little shade humor. Something tells me it's a little late in the day for that.)

When I said the roof caved in on Weiss & Rifkind, Frank, I wasn't kidding. It really did. A couple of years ago the top floor of the Weiss & Rifkind building on Grand Street suddenly collapsed. That was the floor where all the sewing machines and cutters worked. The fire department would later say that the weight of all those sewing machines going night and day, you could hear them vibrating through the whole building, would prove too much for the old wooden floor. This was just a couple of days before Ike's election. He had come to town for a motorcade that passed our building. I always said it wouldn't have happened if Stevenson had been in the car. I know you were a Stevenson man yourself, weren't you Frank, or was that Betty's influence? I know she was ga-ga for the man with the hole in his shoe. Now Kennedy's got him over at the U.N. I feel sorry for the Commie ambassador and his interpreter; they've got to listen to Adlai whether they like it or not.

It's a crazy world, Francis, is it not? I'm sure you're wondering what happened to all the gang over at Weiss & Co. Well it just so happened that it was the lunch hour and every one of those folks on the third floor had gone on their lunch break. The sewing machines just stood there alone when the whole floor opened up and it rained sewing machines all along Grand Street. The bottom two floors were not quite as empty. One man had a sewing machine needle stuck in his leg but except for shrapnel like that, thank God no one was hurt. But the business, Frank, never recovered. That's when I wrote you that note asking for the loan. You were the official pal for life when that beautiful check floated my way. Frank, I swear, it fluttered out of that Sands Hotel envelope as pretty as a butterfly and into my ever appreciative mitt. Joe D. would've been proud of the way I caught that thing. Though I never understood why it was a Sands Hotel check signed by a Mr. Jack Entratter. No note or anything. But you were probably thinking about the mitzvah of an anonymous gift. Frank, I never realized how deep you were until I received that check drawn on the Sands Hotel. In fact it's partly the reason I got married at the Sands. But that seems like a long time ago. And that's another story, one for the road as you would say. So I'll save it and try to forward my next dispatch from the front, Ernie Pyle style, when you're at the Fountainbleu. You're still the only guy I know who has to sing for his supper. Catch a mermaid for me, pal.

Yours,

The world's biggest
Finkie

Dear Frank,

Well, Pally, as Joe E. Lewis used to say, "A friend in need is a pain in the ass." But not to me, Francis. I saw the reviews of the show at the Copa. What does Harriet Van Horne (accent on the horny if you ask me) know about singing in a saloon? Who the hell is she to talk about your "attitude"—Harriet Van Horne wears socks to bed and you can quote me.

I thought perhaps my last missive might've thrown you off your game coming as it did just before your opening at the Copa. Well, maybe failure's gone to my head but I thought an apology might be in order in case my story about the Weiss & Rifkind disaster left you hanging.

It was a dark day indeed, friend of my bosom, when while driving home I hear on the news about the collapse. You hear about all sorts of terrible miseries but at the end of it you can still go home and put your head on the pillow and sleep the sleep of kings. Now don't get me wrong, pal, Finkie doesn't own a heart of stone. It's just that you rarely hear a sad story twice, but when it happens to you, you live it over and over again. The sun rises and sets on the same piece of bad news. That pillow with the goose feathers starts to look very far away, like some tropical paradise to which you've lost the map.

I thought of you then, Francis. I probably should've thought about Jill and the kid but I didn't. I thought about what it must've been like for you twelve years ago when you suffered that throat hemorrhage—terrified that you'd lose your voice—and when you were voted the least cooperative star and Sammy remembered seeing you alone on the street, wrapped in a big overcoat, the saddest man in New York. I felt that way, Francis, coming home to Jill the day Weiss & Rifkind collapsed.

There I was on the edge of an abscess. Blinking. Life is one headline after another, isn't it, pal? All of a sudden I felt like drinking again, like when I heard that ABC pulled the plug on your new show. I thought to myself, that could be me after Mr. Weiss decided to sell what was left of Weiss & Rifkind. But Jill was a saint, Frank. After months of worrying at the track about what to do, she put down her foot with a strong hand and told me in no uncertain terms what it was I should do. Get a job. An ill wind blows no good or so they say, and so I decided the Weiss & Rifkind disaster was a blessing in disguise. A deus ex machina, as the Greeks say, to get out of the shade business for a while.

As you know, Frank, I'm something of an artiste myself. I used to draw caricatures at the Palisades during the summer when I was a kid. I always wanted to be a painter but could never work up the nerve to tell the folks—this was before we were orphaned. My old man used to be afraid I'd grow up to be a painter. I think he thought that in order to be an artist you had to be a little light in the loafers. He also said they never made any money and usually went crazy. That was enough for me. But after I lost my job with the company, that's when I started to work at Mama Joe's on those caricatures. She hung them all up on the wall, all over the place. It looked like the Louvre instead of a clam bar which is what it was. Sardi's it wasn't. But I was happy as one of those proverbial clams until the health department came in and said my sketches were a health hazard. Apparently, because I did all the framing myself at the restaurant while eating the free dinner Mamma Joe offered before the place got busy, the inspector noticed some food that must've accidentally stuck to the glass in one of the frames. It's true there was a terrible odor coming from somewhere but we could never figure out what it was. We thought a rodent or a cat maybe had gotten stuck in the wall and died. Who would've thought it was my drawings that stunk the place up? So that was the beginning and the ending of my artiste career. You see you're not the only one who suffers for his art, Pal.

Your "Clyde,"

Finkie

Dear Father Frank,

I have a confession to make. I had an unkind thought about you the day my marriage went south. I thought somehow you were responsible, indirectly of course, for Jill's leaving and taking Nancy Ava with her (Yes, Francis, we named her after your first two successful marriages). You see, it all has to do with my brother Myron and the Rat Pack dream.

Lately, I've been having dreams about being with you and the boys—Joey Bishop introduces you and Dean as "the Italian bookends" while wheeling the breakfast bar onto the stage.

"Well, here they are folks—Haig and Vague. . . . In a few minutes they'll start telling you about some of the good work the Mafia is doing." A few minutes later Sammy Davis appears in my dream and throws a lemon meringue pie in Joey's face, then all of a sudden Dean staggers out, picks up Sammy and hands him over to you, saying, "This is an award that just arrived for you from the NAACP." Toward the end of the show Peter Lawford-in-law and Joey Bishop stroll across the stage wearing boxer shorts and tuxedo jackets.

The place goes crazy. But Frank, here's where I go crazy in the Rat Pack dream. I'm at ringside sitting with my brother and with Jilly and his wife. Myron starts looking a little green around the gills and says he's going to go out and get some air.

I follow him outside and walk him around the block a few times. "The desert air is good for you," I keep saying. But somehow it doesn't help his breathing. His asthma keeps getting worse while the whole time I'm feeling guilty because I want to be back in the main room where I can hear you introducing me from ringside.

But I'm not in the room! I'm outside holding Myron's hand on the strip while the whole clan is calling my name, "Finkie, Finkie. Where are you, you sunuvabitch?" Then I hear you say, "This guy's a real cheech." I wanted to kill that brother of mine. Finally, when Myron's asthma attack subsided, I raced back into the Copa Room of the Sands, but it was completely empty. Except for Myron who sat on a banquette in the back of the room with a smile on his face.

He's always been my problem, Frank. Ever since our folks died I've looked after the guy. He's only two years younger than me. But he rode in the ambulance with my mother after her stroke and held her hand all the way into the hospital where she died. Myron was one good looking guy, Frank, with a great big chest like Robert Mitchum, the chest of a swimmer, which is what he was up in the Catskills as a lifeguard. The young Westchester mice really went for him—even the older, married dames liked to corner him on the dance floor and push their personal life right in front of him. He was like catnip, my brother. But he never married. I think the last time he went on a date was during the Suez crisis. Once Jill and I saw him with a woman in a restaurant on Lexington Avenue and when he saw us, Myron practically dragged his date out the front door. He didn't approve of my marrying Jill either, Frank. And for the first few years of our marriage I kept our marriage a secret. And I continued to live with Myron and "commute" to be with Jill. She knew all about it, Frank, and she put up with an awful lot. But eventually she got sick of it and told me to choose between the two of them.

I was saved from having to make a choice when Nancy Ava came along. But as the lawyers like to say, it set a bad precedent, Frank. I've called Myron up every night of my married life. Close the door to my office at home and go into a little conference with my brother. I almost feel like he's trying to involve me in a conspiracy against Jill and Nancy Ava. But that's where you come in, Francis. When I told Jill about my recurring Rat Pack dream, she said that if I would care to notice, that only Myron was in that empty room, and that that's the only person I ever really cared about. Jill said she couldn't compete with Myron and the mother-in-law she never knew.

Frank, that hit me like one of Tami Mauriello's left hooks. The next thing I knew I was picking up my mail at the Holiday Inn and meeting lawyers for lunch. . . . My Nancy Ava's grown up to be a pretty cute little mouse herself, wearing long white gloves to her school dance. I hope they play "Nancy (with the laughing face)." I even took a picture of her with one of those instant cameras. It was almost eerie, Frank, watching Nancy's picture showing up from nothing. It reminded me of Peter Hurkos, the guy who goes around taking pictures of ghosts, like a woman who died a hundred years ago coming down the stairs in her own house. Nancy Ava's picture looked like that for a while, until it came through and you could see her perfectly, turning her head and looking toward the window in the living room, almost, Frank, as if she was looking out toward the future, which certainly had to be better than what we were going through then. The night she left for her dance, Jill and I just stood around her like a couple of Spanish chaperones, I forget what they're called. The funny thing is I didn't think much about Nancy Ava or Jill that night, Frank. But I did think a lot about my old man. I thought about his coming home one day with his suit jacket messed up with blood. His nose was broken. He sold pretzels for a while dressed up in a suit like he was going to work on Wall Street or something. It was brown with white stripes. It's ironed into my brain, Frank. Some jerk started to give him a hard time, and this was during the really hard times, and he just lost it and the two men started to go at it, and this guy broke my father's nose, Frank. He always snored after that. My mother hated the way his nose looked. I liked it. He reminded me of Benny Leonard, the fighter. I had pictures of Benny Leonard in my scrapbook so his broken nose suited me fine. So for some reason, Frank, I started to think about all this the night Nancy Ava stepped out of the house in those long gloves and, I guess, took my youth away.

No more pretzel stands for the Finkelsteins, Francis. Levelor blinds (have you seen them anywhere?) is a tide that lifts all Finkelstein boats. So, no sob sister act for me. And as far as my love life—if they take Magic Fingers out of this hotel I'm a dead man.

Yours till Dean sobers up,

Finkie

Frankie My Friend,

What can I say? I'm so grateful that you got Frankie Jr. back in one piece. I've never known anyone personally I've admired as much as you who had someone close to them kidnapped. And it's a terrible feeling, Frank, let me tell you. The gods have not been smiling on us lately, Francis. What does the Big Boy want from us? First Kennedy and then just two weeks later Frankie is scooped up in Tahoe while eating his dinner. I heard that it was a couple of punks posing as room service that broke in and took Frank away at the point of a gun. Really, pal, it was the worst fifty-four hours of my life. I didn't know what to do for you and Nancy. I even put away all the albums, vowing never to play them until Frank Jr. was safely returned to us. Thank God he was released unharmed. (I really missed those records.) What a terrible feeling to want to do something for a pal and not know how to help. I felt like an indecisive Jack Ruby. The Jews already have one of those, Frank. It was strange wasn't it, Francis, that the kidnappers asked for only $240,000. I'm sure you would've given millions. I thought of offering myself as collateral but then I had the problem of who would console the family of Milton Fine.

You see, Frank, Milton was an old friend of mine from the Weiss & Rifkind days. He went through a divorce around the same time Jill and I split up and so we became even closer friends due to our mutual miseries. Although Milton's wife ran off with my old friend Hangars (You know Julie Chalfin, the bridal veil king?). Anyhoo, Milton and I were old friends. Milton once made me promise to look after his two kids if anything should happen to him. He wasn't sick, Francis, just the kind of guy who always owed people money. Sometimes not very nice people Milton was into—for more scratch than I care to mention. So he could never be quite sure who he was dealing with. But he loved those two kids. I can't for the life of me remember their names. They were cockamamie names like the kind they give to kids nowadays. I'm grateful, Frank, that according to the actuarial tables, we're not going to have to meet a lot of octogenarians with names like Heather and Glen. No foresight in those names, Francis! So of course I gave Milton my solemn promise to look after Fric and Frac. Even though it's a little hard as he's got one upstate at some kind of military school and the little one lives with her mother who works all day at a high class beauty parlor in Great Neck and so parks the kid with a neighbor who, it seems to me, Frank, spends all day entertaining salesmen from Fuller Brush. But I digress.

So one day Milton (as is his wont) goes to Pilgrim State Hospital to visit his cousin Frieda who's been in the booby hatch ever since the day after her wedding night. Milton is like that, Frank. He's kind of my Jilly. The Rock of Gibraltar meets the Berlin Wall, that's Milton. So he's visiting his cousin Frieda when poor Milton drops dead of a heart attack. His heart just attacked him and he fell back down in his chair right in Frieda's room. Well, Frieda being cooped up in a pyscho ward practically her whole life without any visitors likes having Milton around, even though as the days pass he's not much company. Finally, someone realizes that Milton never quite signed out of the hospital after signing in, so they go to look for him and find him in Frieda's room, a little worse for wear and dead as the Greek language.

But Milton's troubles weren't over, Frank. In fact, they were just beginning. It seems that Milton had secretly married a black woman named Felicia, a real serious young dame who was ga-ga for the Catholic Church. She decided to have Milton buried as a Catholic, with priests and incense and Jesus on the cross looking down on Milton in his coffin. Milton's parents almost had matching aneurysms when they found out they'd have to go to church to bury their son. Old man Fine was a cantor, for crissake, up in Riverdale. So who gets the call to work things out, the week of Frankie Jr.'s abduction? Your favorite manufacturers rep.

So I went to see Felicia in her apartment near Queens Boulevard. She offered me lots of Milton's stuff—his shoes, his golf clubs, stuff like that, some of his favorite ties. Needless to say, with the exception of some of the ties I begged off. I told her to give it all to Goodwill or donate it to a retirement home— I knew of one in the Bronx, we used to call the Exacta Arms, due to all the elderly bookies and bettors who wound up living there. (They'd sneak bets out with the Puerto Rican orderlies.) It was like Santa Anita only with wheelchairs.

After much hand holding I positioned myself near the Kleenex box in order to reach out strategically for a tissue with which to help her with the waterworks which I knew would eventually come, first in a trickle or two and then watch out, Niagara Falls here we go!

I should have been Kennedy's choice at the U.N., Francis, for I talked Felicia into allowing Milton's parents to have a private service at Maimonides, and then she could do with Milt whatever the hell she wanted—she could have him declared a saint for all I cared. St. Milton of Hewlett—the patron saint of discount.

Well, Frank, here you are getting over the biggest fright of your life and I've got you thinking about Pilgrim State Hospital and the last rites. We should be cracking open a bottle of Cold Duck now that Frankie Jr.'s back. I heard about that nut who plays the piano, Oscar Levant, saying that if Frank Jr. was kidnapped it must've been done by music critics. What a sick guy. A real stinker. If I ever see that fruitcake I'll give him a piece of your mind.

I'm glad that a man's best pal is happy tonight and that Frankie Jr. gets to sleep in his own bed.

Yours,

Fink

Dear Frank,

You'll forgive a pal who's trying to break into the business a little late in life, but I've written a play for you, Francis. It's called "The Kidnapping of Frank Sinatra, Jr." You might want to think about playing Frankie Jr., so I thought I'd let you warm up for the part of Terry Malloy in *On the Waterfront*. I'm glad you told "Mumbles Brando" to call you "Mr. Sinatra" the next time you ran into him at Chasen's.

Someone without your sophistication, your élan, if you pardon my French, pal, might think this play a shameful exploitation of a near-tragedy, but I know you better than that, Francis. In fact the entire thing is told in a flashback while you are in your car driving to the designated drop-off point with the ransom money. We flash all the way back to the first time you cut Frankie Junior's hair, going up to the point when he struck out on his own to sing for his supper at Tahoe where he was abducted.

There are some very intense scenes between both Frankie and his kidnappers, and a split-screen approach to you and Nancy reacting to the news. I think you're really going to like it, Frank. In fact, you might be interested to know that I had a burst of inspiration for the ending while I was in Los Angeles for a trade show. I was driving on the San Diego Freeway when I realized that Frankie was let go somewhere along the Mulholland Drive exit. Needless to say, it sent a shiver down my spinal column to be finishing the play in a car, so close to the actual spot where so much of the action in the play takes place. When Frankie stumbles out of the bushes and on to someone's driveway, after the kidnappers have fled, he notices a newspaper lying on the front lawn dated Dec. 11, 1963—one day before your birthday, Frank.

Two days ago I received a letter from Mrs. Kennedy, thanking me for taking the time to express my sorrow over the death of President Kennedy. It wasn't a letter exactly, Francis, but a white card with a black border around it, and printed out in a kind of wedding invitation handwriting was her note to me. If that's a sample of her handwriting, Francis, she is truly a great lady. When I opened up the letter, I thought at first that Jill had remarried. It looked so much like a wedding invitation, only it was a wedding invitation to a funeral.

I know how heartbroken you were when Bobby Kennedy

pulled the plug on his brother's staying with you in Palm Springs. It must've been galling for you to have the president staying at Bing's house just a few miles up the road from your house. And that, after all the trouble you went through to expand the place!

A man can never tell, Pal, what's going to happen, or not happen, under his own roof. I know you can relate to this story, Frank, especially after all you've been through with Frank Jr.

Jill and I were worried about our daughter when she began to be afraid that the roof of our house was going to fall in on her. At first, we thought it might've been some delayed reaction to what happened to the Weiss & Rifkind Building in New York and the trauma that caused around here. But eventually it got so bad that she could only sleep at her friend's house. We hardly ever saw her. We finally took Nancy to a headshrinker, a guy named Bushmiller (who I quickly re-named Bullshitter and Bill-Me-Will-Ya). He told us that as young as Nancy was, she had been picking up on all the trouble Jill and I were having. Of course, the kid was right, Frank. The roof was going to cave in. I had a hole in my head (as you would say) that everyone could see through except me.

So now I'm spending a lot of time at the Hilton on Seventh Avenue, the one across from Radio City Music Hall where I used to take Jill and Nancy to see the Christmas show. (I know what you're thinking; what are six Jew feet doing on line for the Christmas show? But Nancy loved seeing all the animals onstage, and she had a crush on one of the Three Wise Guys, the guy holding the myrrh.) So there I am holed up at the Hilton with my kid. We had to take her out of the house just so she could get some sleep.

So I'm trying to work, take care of Nancy, and dodge crabby phone calls from Jill, while sidewalk Santas start blooming up out of the cracks in the sidewalk to spread their nerve-wracking good cheer.

One night, I noticed, Nancy had taken one of our photo albums from the house. It was the first one Jill had kept after our wedding and the honeymoon at Niagara Falls. The pictures of Jill in that yellow raincoat they give you with that fisherman's hat, the whole thing straight out of Morton Salt, just broke me up. Frank, the photos still look wet. One picture of Jill standing on Peace Bridge, between New York and Canada, leaning against the viewfinder, with its big empty eyes that open up for a quarter and let you see everything so close you could drink it, that picture really tore my heart out. To think that we went over the falls together not in a barrel but with a suitcase and with so much hope in the future and now my kid's afraid to sleep in her own house and my wife looks back at me from Niagara Falls, 20,000 leagues under the sea. The scourge of marriage has come out of its cave beneath the falls, Francis. I'm listening a lot to "In the Wee Small Hours of the Morning" these days. My pillow's a land mine. I don't dare fall asleep. My phrasing's off tonight, Frank.

Yours,

Finky

Dear Frank,

I'm so sorry you lost Cal-Neva. It was a beautiful spot, Francis. Tahoe will never be the same. It was a dream come true. It was Sinatraland. I'm only sorry we were never there at the same time. (Am I right, Frank, did you or did you not give your Nancy's husband Tommy Sands a shot at the show-room?)

Our Nancy wanted us to take her up to Cal-Neva to see Tommy perform. But I believe that the Sands kid couldn't quite make it at those high altitudes, so you pulled the plug on him after the first show. I took the family up anyway, Frank. It was like old home week. I couldn't believe all the fellas you had up there, Francis. Uncle Ruby—Irwin Rubenstein of Ruby's Dunes in Palm Springs—was running the dining room, and another nafka I hadn't seen since I was knee-high to Rubirosa was friend Skinny D'Amato of the 500 Club. When I saw Skinny running the showroom, I knew I was home. And then those bastards at the gaming commission took it all away. Cal-Neva was Sinatraland writ large. (See what a little night school does to a guy?) I pointed out to Jill and Nancy Ava how the joint reflected your ideas, even your favorite colors—beige, orange and brown. I explained how every detail down to the light switches and every employee from the maitre d' to the kids parking the cars was hand picked by Frank Sinatra himself. To say that you worked hard on making Cal-Neva live up to your dreams would not begin to approximate your effort. The thing about Cal-Neva, the thing those goombahs at the commission don't understand was that Cal-Neva not only offered music, gambling, the bright lights and roulette wheels of Vegas or Monte Carlo, but it offered night life and razzle-dazzle juxtaposed with giant trees, clean air, outdoor sports and purple mountains. God, we were happy there.

What's with these G-men? They've got the Mafia on the brain. Every saloon singer coming up knew the old bootleggers. My cousin Harry Schwartz used to earn a few bucks picking up Al Capone's laundry when Harry was a punk kid just learning how to smoke a cigar. Some of these Mobsters, I hasten to add, are not Italian but Jewish. Are you listening, Meyer? I remember looking at the signatures on the Famous Door—you remember Lenny Hayton's old place—where all the famous patrons signed the front door as they came in. Well, someone should read off the names. The Duke of Windsor's got his John Hancock right beside Sammy G's. What hurts the most, Frank, is that we can't share the disappointment with you. You're the one who always tries to be the big man, you won't let anybody else help you out of a hole. I haven't felt this inadequate since the breakup of your marriage to Ava. Remember, Frank, when you bury anger you only wind up carrying a grudge. I know how it feels when you can't afford to get mad and they won't let you get even. There's a Latin expression that goes something like don't let the bastards grind you down. I had an uncle who had that sign above his bed. I noticed it hanging there the day he died. Even though I had been in that apartment a thousand times, I never noticed it before then. But it's a good motto, don't you think, Francis?

Cal-Neva is dead, long live Cal-Neva! Your ever lovin' pal,

The Finkster

Dear Frank,

Ocean's 11 is a masterpiece. I'm heartbroken, if a guy can get heartbroken, that I wasn't available to make it Ocean's 12. When you, Peter, Conte, Tamiroff—you're all sitting in the chapel and the money gets cremated, I had to get a drink just to calm myself down. What an ending, Frank! It reminds me of something I read recently where Elizabeth Taylor was talking about Richard Burton on the set of *Cleopatra*. You know what she called him? The Frank Sinatra of Shakespeare. But after seeing you as Danny Oceans, I can safely say Mr. William Shakespeare doesn't deserve to carry your jockstrap. It all reminded me of what Bogart had to say about how if you could only stay away from the broads, and devote more time to developing yourself as an actor, you'd be one of the best in the business. It's true of me too, Frank. I've been offered the presidency of at least two shade giants—Suzy Day and the Monster, as we call it, The Merchant of Venetian Blinds, Co. But a little practical joke seemed to have backfired on me involving the then Chairman of the Board—the other chairman of the board—Ira Oppenheimer.

We were all at a trade show in Chicago, the Merchandise Mart, owned by old Joe Kennedy, by the way. We were staying at the Parker House, where Ira was going to interview me about running his company. It would've been a very big step for me, Frank. So I thought, what would Frank do in a situation like this, in order to make a big impression? So during the interview out on Ira Oppenheimer's terrace I blew up Mr. Oppenheimer's shoes. You see, Frank, all during the trade show Ira had wanted some new shoes. All the other salesman got so tired of hearing about it that I decided to set off some cherry bombs in Ira's new shoes and they blew at least twenty feet in the air. All the reps were watching from down below. We were hysterical.

Ira offered the job to his son-in-law. It's like Nancy Ava once said to her school guidance counselor, "You travel with Dad, you see every jail in the world." She was kidding, Francis, of course. But in fact, I didn't want the responsibility of running a big corporation. I was holding out for the Rat Pack to draft me into active duty. I want to breathe the air of the Summit. *Ocean's 11, Sergeant's Three, Robin and the Seven Hoods.* I want to see Angie Dickinson naked before I die, Francis.

For a while I even had my own Rat Pack going. On one occasion we all flew down to Miami. We checked into the Fountainbleu while Sammy was playing there. Three pals of mine from the shade business and a colored guy, a real sweetheart, who's married to our maid, Sophie. We were all set. Morris, an ex-Englishman (our Peter), was up on the fifteenth floor, sharing a penthouse with Mr. Smith, Sophie's husband. Down on the seventh floor was Blinkie, whose sister recently married the director Martin Ritt. Blinkie works for the Hoffritz knife people, and has to go to Germany a lot, which he hates. He wants to be in show business and works on a comedy routine every chance he gets. He calls it "The Act." I tell him it would be an act of mercy to stop doing it. He's our Joey Bishop. He got the name Blinkie due to a nervous tic he developed of fits of uncontrolled blinking. Sometimes, Frank, it looks like he's signaling to ships when he looks out at the ocean from the balcony. When they put Blinkie in a regular room, when we were all in the fifteenth-floor penthouse, we pulled a Frank—"If our friend Blinkie isn't in a suite on the fifteenth floor in five minutes," I told the manager, "we'll be out of this hotel and Sammy Davis tells me they'll be no show."

All of a sudden six bellboys run into Blinkie's room while he's in the middle of shaving his legs, and grab his clothes, his shoes, his toiletries, and practically carried him into a suite. You may walk through a situation and leave a few bodies strewn about, Francis, but I think those guys knocked each other out trying to get out of the way. You have to be willing to face the dark side of Frank Sinatra, I tell people. Sometimes, in the life of a man, you have to be willing to visit the dark side of his moon.

I almost fell in love at the Fountainbleu that year, Frank. That was the year Jerry was filming *The Bellboy* at the hotel. At Sammy's show, I met a sweet young kid who had a small part in Jerry's movie. Her name was Karyn Kupcinet. She was Irv

Kupcinet's daughter. She was an intense little mouse, Frank, a brunette who wore eyeglasses in her spare time. She had the eyes, the face really, of a Persian cat. She told me she had done a few Perry Mason episodes and that Jerry had personally chosen her without knowing anything about her being Kup's kinder. The boys all kidded me about spending a whole evening listening to Carl Sandburg records on her hi-fi. She liked the poem Sandburg read on Ed Sullivan about Chicago, city of the big shoulders. Anyway, Francis, you could imagine how stunned I was by the story coming out of L.A. the week of the Kennedy assassination, that Karyn was found dead in her apartment off Sunset. I couldn't believe it. Somehow, Frank, it was more terrible or at least more real than President Kennedy's assassination. Sweet Karyn Kupcinet, found dead on the couch with the TV on. Someone had left a copy of a book *The Tropic of Cancer* by that guy Henry Miller—that guy could teach us a thing or two, Frank. Anyway, the cops didn't know what to make of poor Karyn's death. One of the suspects was an ex-boyfriend of hers, Andrew Prine. Ever hear of this guy, Frank? He's a young actor who apparently had visited Karyn sometime before the murder. Not many people, including the police, were paying too much attention to it, due to the fact that the whole country was in mourning for the president. Karyn wrote me a few short, sweet letters, Frank. You'd even think to read them that we had done the naughty deed up there on the fifteenth floor, but we hadn't. Just Carl Sandburg and some champagne with that great ocean keeping what the eggheads call sidereal time.

They never found her killer, Frank. Though to this day Irv Kupcinet and Lew Wasserman, Irv's old friend, would pay a king's ransom to know what really happened to that sweet kid.

Eventually, Blinkie and I had a falling out. I won't bore you with the details, but suffice it to say that there were a couple of misunderstandings. Not the least of which was Blinkie's refusal to show my play about Frankie Jr.'s kidnapping to his brother-in-law Mr. Ritt. So I had no choice, Frank, but to stop talking to Blink. According to Blinkie, he was a scapegoat for my disappointment over Karyn. Perhaps this is so. But Blinkie should have come to me about his feelings, not to the other guys. He chose not to argue it out like a man. He simply moved unprotestingly out of my life. It's like what your Nancy says about you, Frank, "You've got to face Frank Sinatra. Battle it out. You can't be so in awe of him that you're awed right out of a relationship." Ring-a ding. We can all see a little more clearly now that Blinkie's out of the picture. It's basic. It's right and wrong. That's the only rule. I've got that raincoat slung over my shoulder, pal, but the trouble is it never rains in Miami Beach.

Your pal,

Finkie

Dear Frank,

I just put down my trumpet (my asthma inhaler) in order to send salutations to the Master. *Sinatra and Strings* has changed everything, Frank. The only question left, Francis, is what do *you* listen to when *you* want to score?

Myron doesn't get it, Frank. He doesn't understand what it means to live your life according to Sinatra's rules of engagement. If I had been honest with Myron, Frank, if I had only been straight with him about the marriage to Jill, I wouldn't be sitting here reading hundreds of clippings about disasters, troubles in Israel, and the discovery of new diseases. Maybe I haven't told you about Myron and his clippings, Frank. Well, I think you should know. As an only child you didn't have to contend with a brother's love or his jealousy. Myron seemed jealous of everything I ever did, Frank. When Jill was pregnant, I started to get newspaper articles that Myron would cut out of the papers about Thalidamide babies, and something they called crib death, about babies who die in their sleep. Real tragedies. And some of these were marked "SAVE" in red pen. When Jill and I were about to close on our house I came home one day to a manila envelope bursting with articles about a rise in home foreclosures and absolute horror stories about people who lost everything when their homes burned down, along with brochures about home insurance.

Now, if you told Myron that these stories were not helpful, that, in fact, it only made things harder for us, he would act hurt and pout that he was only trying to help and don't we want his help in these big decisions, which of course we didn't.

Well, Frank, instead of telling Myron to go sit in a hole and mind his own business, to go out and get his own life, I dutifully read all the articles, and I even save the ones marked

"SAVE" and handed them back to him when we met for lunch at the Bluebird, a diner up in Riverdale. I know that you're thinking, Frank, "Cool it. Back Off. Forget it." You give people an argument and then they get a lot of press. "This guy's looking for a hassle, and you're saying to yourself, 'Ignore him.'" But Frank, he's my brother. You'd give a guy your dinner, if you liked him. The truth is, Frank, I don't really like Myron all that much. But he's my parents' kid, even if he is a schmuck. You know, when we were little, I remember, not far from Tony the shoe-maker's (I think your mother Dolly brought all the Sinatra shoes to Tony) I once passed Myron on the street banging some kid's head against the curb because he owed Myron a nickel. If I had lived my life with Myron according to Frank's rules, I wouldn't have gotten sucked into Myron's meshugas. I should've gotten all this off my chest years ago, and you know something, Frank, it would've helped Myron, too, to get on with his life. Maybe find a girl, get married. I felt sorry for him, so I never let him grow up. Anytime I read that you've been rude, Francis, I tell myself, and this is the God's honest truth, I think, as Sammy would say, the cat deserved it. That's the difference between Frank and everybody else, I tell people, where you and I or even Dean might put up with what a guy did, Frank won't. He'll say it right to you, "Don't do that," because that's his unbreakable rule. I remember talking to one guy, Frank, who saw you at Don the Beachcomber's. He came up to you while you were having dinner, and he asked you if he could take one picture of you at the table. You were very agreeable and said something like, "O.K.

Pal, take one." But the guy kept snapping his camera and replacing the bulbs in the flash, and so you lost it. I think he said you started yelling at him, "Hey, hey, that's enough already! You asked for one." It's that basic. Myron had one picture coming to him after our folks died and we were on our own. But he kept snapping away and I never confronted him that first time and so now I'm so used to Myron's flashbulbs in my face, I don't even blink anymore.

Yours till Johnson wins in a landslide,

Fink

Dear Frank,

I owe you an apology. The world is always pounding on you and here I am writing you these letters like some sob sister. I'm in L.A. for a week, visiting my Uncle Dave. You might've seen my uncle in a couple of pictures. He was an expert with a bullwhip. Something he learned to do in Russia as a young man traveling with a small circus. He was one of eleven children. Some of them came to America and most of those settled in New York. The others made their home in Palestine. But Dave Finkelstein was different. He wanted to be a movie star. He looks a lot, Francis, like Yul Brynner or Mr. Clean. The women in these small Russian towns were crazy about him. In Los Angeles he found work in silent pictures, using his bullwhip, knocking a cigarette out of a woman's mouth, playing the taskmaster in a slave ship. Dave would send photographs of himself to his family in Palestine, autographed like pictures from a movie studio. "To Leah, from her handsome brother. Dave."

But Uncle Dave was doomed in talking pictures, Frank. He had a thick Jewish accent, and his truly amazing skill with a bullwhip was the only thing he could do in the movies. So his career was limited to the odd walk on. The other day I went to visit him on the set of *Silk Stockings*. When I arrived on the set, Uncle Dave was sleeping in a small trailer in the dark. He was naked, his barrel chest moving up and down while a small fan oscillated on the floor.

"Kom in, Vinkie," Uncle Dave said. "But you must be veddy, veddy quiet. I am between tecks. You know vat a teck es, Vinkie?" Frank, the guy never even got up from his cot to greet me. He was sprawled out there like Lawrence Fucking Olivier with gorilla hair. The great artiste, Uncle Dave. He's got one scene in the entire movie, where Cyd Charisse stops dancing in a Russian work camp when Uncle Dave walks through as a Soviet inspector. He doesn't even have any lines. Last year I took Nancy Ava to see Uncle Dave on the Art Linkletter show. He did a few stunts like lifting a cigarette out of Art Linkletter's mouth and removing, with his bullwhip, the buttons on a sailor's coat.

Uncle Dave wanted Nancy Ava to sit on his lap when we drove to the studio. Nancy later said that it made her feel uncomfortable. She said she thought Uncle Dave liked to pull up her skirt in the back of the car and talk about what beautiful legs she had and how she should go into show business with those legs. I felt like slugging the bastard. But I didn't do anything about it. I felt badly for the old guy. He lives in an efficiency apartment on Franklin Street in L.A. He kept telling us about all the stars he has lunch with at Musso & Frank's. He was really laying it on for Nancy's sake. He asked her if she would like to meet William Frawley. Uncle Dave said he and Frawley were great friends. But when we went into Musso & Frank's with Uncle Dave, only the counterman seemed to pay him any mind. He had a shrimp cocktail and a scotch and soda. Nancy cried when we dropped him off at his apartment. She said she didn't know why she was crying, that she didn't even really like Uncle Dave.

Well, Francis, the fifteen-minute intermission is over. It's about time for you to come back onstage with your Jack Daniel's in a glass, for the real magic to begin. You see, that's how I tell time. Not by the wristwatch Jill gave me for our 10th and last wedding anniversary, but by your stage time. It's my internal Sinatra clock. Thirty minutes strolling the stage like an Italian poet making it up as you go along. Then, the fifteen minutes off. Then precisely fifteen later, you're back for two hours and forty minutes, depending on your mood, the chemistry of the crowd. You're the only one, Frank, who can be onstage for four hours and still have a hundred songs left. I've got a hundred stories to tell you, pal. But they'll have to wait till the supper crowd goes home. I am truly one of the most fortunate of men, because I have the chairman of the board here in my chest, not in the brain, but the chest. I know instinctively now what

Frank would do in a given sitch. Like you, Frank, I know a lot of people, but no one knows me. Pardon my philosophy, Francis, I just thought you oughta hear it from a pal.

Finky

Dear Frank,

How the hell did all these people get in my room? Isn't that what you used to say when you walked onstage at the Sands? Well, that's what I said, Frank, when I opened my baby browns and saw a roomful of white coats, Jill, and some other suspicious characters standing around my bed in what looked a little too much like a hospital room. Apparently, Frank, I conked out while watching the electric parade in Disneyland. The family was reunited for Nancy Ava's 13th birthday and when Cleopatra's coach (No, pal, make that Sleeping Beauty's limo. Nancy gets to fact-check all my letters to her godfather) pulled up I just checked out. The next thing I know I'm looking up at a crowd of eight-year-olds. I felt like that glass bottom boat Nancy Ava made me go on, even though I can't swim and have my own hallucinations, the hell with Disneyland.

I knew it couldn't be anything too serious because I saw Jill and a nurse laughing when I came to in that hospital room. Apparently, Francis, my bird was sky high. It looked like Lawrence of Arabia had been camping out in the middle of my bed. Usually I take great pride in my hard-ons, Frank, but this was ridiculous. So this nurse, name Miss Stillwagon, leans over and gives the bird a flick with her finger, the one with the wedding ring on it, and I go down quicker than the *Andrea Doria*. I still have a purple welt where my purple welt should be. But I wasn't in the hospital, Frank, for being priapic in Disneyland. The doctor said I had hypoglycemia, in other words low blood sugar. I can make light of it now, Frank, but I really thought the big G was calling in his chips and without consulting you, Frank!

I wasn't ready to visit the Big Casino, Francis. Nancy Ava is still just a kid and Jill looked almost young enough to be my wife. But seriously, pal, I could've married her all over again, right there in Disneyland. Maybe Bluebeard could've married us on Treasure Island.

I half expected to see you standing over me at Mt. Sinai, Frank. I remember how good you were to Lee J. Cobb after he had his heart attack. I remember thinking at the time what a (you should pardon the expression) fink Cobb was to name people in front of the House Un-American Activities Committee. From what I heard he had almost no friends left in Hollywood after that and that he was on the edge of bankruptcy when you made your move to help the poor bastard.

I mean you took the guy into your own home and paid his medical bills. You did it without even waiting to be thanked. Francis, you're like the fucking Lone Ranger.

I can just imagine you and Lee J. Cobb sitting out on the patio under the stars at Palm Springs, having long talks about life and death. I just don't know how you seem to understand how hard it is sometimes to keep on going, how elusive the will to live can be. I guess you have to scrape bottom before you can appreciate life and start living again. That's why, Frank, I'm writing to you now, in the hope that you might extend yourself yet one more time to someone in need—the kind of need, Francis Albert, you yourself have once known.

You have no idea, Francis, what this hypoglycemia is costing me. This isn't a hospital, Frank, it's a gold mine! I'd have to have shades in every E. J. Korvettes just to pay for the x-rays. My room-mate here at Mt. Sinai tells me that each diuretic is about 25 cents and the catheter is in the stratosphere. I'm also hooked up to a heart monitor that looks like it belongs in Cape Canaveral (I can't bring myself to call it Cape Kennedy, it's too painful).

Two beds down from me, Frank, is Al Tietelbaum the furri-er He made his mark with those fur covered toilet seats. Al says Bing Crosby, no slob he, ordered an ermine-covered toilet seat covered on both sides (cost: $400). Al says he once covered a television set in skunk for Harry Cohn, because Cohn hated television with a passion.

Everyone says that your comeback has made you even more generous. I hope this is still the case because your pal will have to sell a whole lot of drapery hardware to buy back the blood they took out of me since I've been here. There's an eleventh commandment we have up here in Mt. Sinai, Francis. It goes something like, "Thou Shalt Pay a Friend's Medical Bills Especially When Thou Art Vice President of the Sands and Earning $100,000 a Week When Thou Performeth." If nothing else, Frank, how about sending an aspirin through college?

When Sammy lost his eye in that automobile accident, he tells people in his show how you drove seventy miles from L.A. to San Bernadino Community Hospital, in the rain, to visit with Sammy and insist that he use your house in Palm Springs for his recuperation. So, Frank, leave the key under the mat, I'm coming to Palm Springs. If I don't hear from you I'll just assume it's not a good time and I'll take a rain check from the greatest friend a guy could hope to have.

I remember when Charlie Morrison died back in '57. I know you were too broken up to attend Charlie's funeral. But Jill and I didn't know him well enough to be that broken up, so we went. When Charlie M. passed away, Frank, the Mocambo died with him. I proposed to Jill at the Mocambo, although I had to repeat myself and propose all over again, in the car, because we always had lousy seats at the Mocambo, near the busboy station. The dishes and silverware, to say nothing of the busboys jabbering in Mexican, and Jill couldn't hear my speech, which I prepared with a little help from that book *Tom Jones* by Henry Fielding. Frank, you gotta read this thing, it's like the stuff in *Playboy* only better written. Anyhoo, there's a seduction scene in there which I practically recited to Jill right there in the Mocambo with the crashing plates. I know she wanted to buy the ring herself, so I bought a cigar and put the cigar ring around her finger. I got that from hearing about President Johnson, and how he got engaged to Lady Bird that way because he was too poor to afford an engagement ring.

So back to Charlie Morrison. Your generosity knew no

bounds even there, Frank. When Charlie died he left Beans, his widow, with a stack of debts and no insurance. Charlie was typical of guys like us, Frank, or I should say everyone except you, Frank. We've got thousands of friends, but about four dollars. But then you arrived, Francis, and saved the day for Beans.

I was so sorry not to get to see you at the Mocambo with Nelson Riddle's orchestra. I mean, here was Frank Sinatra, singing for the first time at a Hollywood nightclub, I don't think you've done it before or since. It must've been New Year's Eve every night. By the end of the two weeks, Beans was able to give Charlie a millionaire's funeral. Even the waiters were able to pay off the mortgages on their homes.

There's no end to your largesse, my liege. When people tell me, "That guy Frank Sinatra is a no good bum," I tell them about the time back in the fifties when Dracula was in the hospital, you know who I mean, the guy who played Dracula was in the hospital because he was a drug addict, and Frank Sinatra sent him a huge basket of delicacies. I remember when Dracula got out of the hospital, how he thanked you for your generosity.

Well, Frank, Dracula wouldn't be interested in my blood. I've got to eat almost all the time now, or else my cabin becomes depressurized. So I get out of Mt. Sinai tomorrow and I'll look for the Golden Calf when I come off that elevator, courtesy of Johnny Concho, a/k/a Frank.

Ever yours,

"Clyde," a/k/a Finky

Dear Frank,

It's Myron, Frank. I'm sorry the guy ever found out I was in the hospital. For weeks now, I've been getting hundreds of clippings and brochures about low blood sugar. He even found out about a monthly bulletin put out by the Hypoglycemia Club of the Bronx—a ten page mimeographed publication called *Weakness*—the magazine devoted to Hypoglycemia. It's really a newspaper for hypochondriacs, Frank. I don't want any part of it.

It's almost as if Myron likes seeing me on the ropes this way. As soon as I got out of the hospital and came back to New Rochelle, Myron was there waiting for me. He wanted to know if I felt well enough to take a walk around the block. He had "things to discuss with me." Frank, the guy's morbidity really started to get to me. I just need to eat six times a day. The guy had my head in a colostomy bag, already. He's always been morbid. Every night I have to listen on the telephone as Myron tells me about all the people in his building who are sick. I don't even know these people. If he wasn't my brother, I would think that he was one of those people who gets some kind of a thrill out of the misfortune of others. How it makes them feel more alive, somehow. Myron really comes to life talking about his friend Howie, who just threw himself off the terrace of his apartment in the Hampshire House, on Central Park South.

Myron was friends with Howie and his brother Tom Lehrer. Tom is getting a lot of attention these days for his satiric songs that he performs at the piano. Songs that make fun of the Vatican and President Johnson. He's like Liberace for eggheads. But Howie wasn't so successful. He tried writing books, great big novels that no one wanted to publish. He had depression, Frank. Two marriages that went south. And one beautiful Sunday afternoon in May, Howie threw himself over the railing of his penthouse and landed on the roof of a taxicab. Tom said later that Howie's chin was ground into dust by the impact. Myron went on for months about the poor guy's death. Trying to "get to the bottom" of why Howie Lehrer destroyed himself like that. But, Frank, Myron only saw the guy a few times a year, usually at dances on Block Island or up in the Catskills. He took the poor bastard's death so personally, you'd think they were brothers. I told Myron he was just using Howie's "accident" to make himself feel badly. He became all upset at my "insinuation" that he didn't care about Howie. He got my point all screwed around. So I just told him to forget about what I said and the two of us went back to talking about the Six Day War.

Myron's never even been to Israel, Frank. He's too cheap to go. But to hear him talk you'd think he was Theodore Herzl himself. I think the real reason Myron doesn't travel to Israel is the relatives. Our father was one of eleven children. Only my father and Uncle Dave, the bullwhip/bullshit artist, came to America—all the other kids traveled from Poland to Palestine. When my father was killed in a car accident in the Bronx on the way to work—a taxicab ran a red light and smashed into Seymour Finkelstein's car and my father's chest was crushed by his own steering wheel—his brothers and sisters in Israel never lifted finger to help us or Miriam, who died not long after that. Her heart was also broken that terrible day. Myron was eleven, I was fifteen.

Myron knows how to hold a grudge, Francis. He's a lot like you in that respect. But I'm a lot like you in another way. It's like your friendship with Dean. I try to keep things light. I don't discuss a guy's girls or who he's going to marry. All I discuss are movies and Sinatra. Sometimes I like to share a phobia or two with a guy I like. The way you told Dean about your fear of heights and then he let on that he couldn't stand elevators. I remember when my buddy, Joel, before he was really a pal of mine, came to me with a long, long face. I thought the guy was gonna recite the Gettysburg Address any minute he looked so gloomy. "What's the matter, Joel?" I asked. It seems, Francis, that Joelie was worried about his bird. All his life he was afraid that his schmuck was outta luck. That his penis came up short. It seems that growing up Joel had an adopted brother who he saw once in the shower, an older kid, who was toweling himself off in an upstairs bathroom. Joel sees this teenage kid, five years older than himself, and thinks, this guy has a great shlong, I've got nothing. It made Joel crazy all these years he's been a bachelor birddogging cute mice.

Well, Frank, I'm not about to compare equipment with this guy, like in that book I just read up at the Concord, *A Moveable Feast* by Hemingway, where he goes into the backroom of some bar in Paris to reassure F. Scott Fitzgerald that his shlong isn't too small. But I sent Joel to my doctor, who examines the nervous schmuck and tells him not to worry, that he's got excellent powers of regeneration, or something like that. (P.S. Privately, Frank, the doc tells me out on the golf course up in the Catskill mountains that while Joel's no Rubirosa, he's fine. He tells me that the guy's real problem is that he's never gotten over the first girl in his life—you guessed it, Frank, his mother.) Which is funnier than you think, Francis, because I've met Joel's mother in Florida and she looks like the love child of Jake LaMotta and Gertrude Stein—you know the Rose is a Rose broad whose got Picassos coming out the kazoo. I prefer your paintings, Frank. You and Tony Curtis are my favorite artists. I've been to Tony Bennett's house and saw a few of his paintings on the wall above his couch. Not bad, really. I know you're turning the guy's career around but maybe while you're at it you can throw in some drawing lessons.

Your pal,

Finkie

Dear Frankie,

I'm becoming a philosopher in my old age, Francis. I'm developing a philosophy of tears. There are the tears you shed in childhood, like when you lose a doll or a mean looking dog runs off with your baseball mitt. Then there are the tears you shed for a real doll. A mouse who breaks your heart. At Weiss & Rifkind, Frank, I once dated a secretary, a Norwegian gal, the daughter of a long line of sailors going back to the original Vikings. She had pictures of all her uncles, and one guy, her grandfather, who looked just like Thor of the comic book, sitting at the head of a giant table. The table didn't have any legs but just sat on two giant boulders at either end. I told Gertrude, that was her name—all her girlfriends at the company called her Trudi; she said it bothered her at first, but now it didn't matter so much, because she knew that people liked her and that it was just too much trouble to correct them all the time—that I could really feel myself falling in love with her. And that I wasn't really sure how she felt about it, being new to this country and all that that entailed. Frank, I felt that mentally, Trudi was reading me my Miranda rights. That my "confession" had merely scared her away. We went out a few more times but then I had the distinct feeling that she was avoiding me

I used to flatter myself that I wasn't the jealous type, Frank. I remember when you shed a few tears for Ava. I think you called her the only woman you ever really loved. Jilly once told us that you sat in your hotel suite at the Dorchester in London and tore up a dozen roses one petal at a time, waiting for Ava to call. Well, this isn't that romantic, Frank. In fact, I'm a little ashamed to tell you, Frank, what I did one night when Trudi cancelled a date with me at the last minute. I smelled a rat, Francis. I was ready to go to the prom with this mouse. Eat Swedish meatballs until the cows came home. I gulped each time she came through the door at work. I had to screw up my courage just to tell her how much I cared about her, even when she wore her hair in those braids that made her look as if she was wearing a hot plate in her hair. It didn't matter to me, Frank. I was in love with a Viking princess on Grand Street who had suffered a bout with polio. But this turns into the "wrong door raid" pretty quickly, Frank. I don't need to remind you how much fun that turned out to be when you and Joltin' Joe kicked in the wrong door looking for Mrs. DiMaggio, only to find a frightened woman screaming in her bed.

Well, I had the right door, Frank. I let myself in to Trudi's apartment. She always kept a key under the welcome mat. I sat in the dark, waiting for her to come home. I was always touched by Trudi's place. It was a bare, little apartment, with a deaf Angora cat I was always allergic to. So I waited for Trudi to come home. And come home she did, with a guy I knew from the office. A sales manager who had, one summer, played a few games at shortstop for the Yankees. Old man Rifkind, the same guy who was always trying to get me to marry his daughter Marcia, gave this shortstop a job with Weiss & Rifkind in the sales department. Personally, I don't think this guy could sell a stethoscope to a medical convention, but Rifkind thought it would be good public relations for the company to hire him. He looked like he was listening to Trudi's heartbeat, from where I sat in the dark. I turned the light on and gave the two lovers the fright of their lives. Then I walked out of the place with a kind of sad, crooked smile on my face. Unlike you, Francis, I didn't have to testify in front of California's Crime Commission about my "wrong door raid." Nor could I say that I was sitting in the car waiting for my pal, DiMag, to come back from looking for his wife. Trudi and I had only had a few quiet nights together. I don't know what possessed me, Frank. I was out of my head for a few moments there, Francis. Come to think of it, I did say one thing as I walked out the door of Trudi's place. I think I said, "I want to thank all those who made this night necessary."

I don't know why that popped into my head. But it did. I think Yogi Berra once said something like that during an event held to honor Yogi in Yankee Stadium. I guess maybe because this guy with Trudi had been a Yankee, it came into my head to say it. Only Sigmund Freud would know the answer to that, Frank, and he's not about to open at the Sands anytime soon.

Speaking of the Sands, Francis, I ran into Doc Stacher, and I made a business deal with the good doctor regarding the Sands. I'll save it for my next missive. But remember, Frank, when you pull the shades down as the sun is coming up in the desert, the room-darkening effect is courtesy of your friend, Finkie, the man who wants to keep the sun out of your eyes in Lost Wages, Nevada.

Fink

Dear Frank,

I'm sleepwalking in Vegas again. Last night I found myself out in the hallway on the other side of the Sands, standing in front of a door behind which I could hear a woman crying quietly to herself, and then what sounded like the voice of a little girl asking her what time it was. I thought I was still dreaming, but the hallway was freezing and the cold must've awakened me. I felt like a real schmuck standing there in my boxer shorts in front of the Danny Thomas suite.

I was in Vegas, Frank, to talk to your friend Mr. Jack Entratter about supplying the Sands with drapery hardware. 1800 bedrooms and they're all going to need curtains, I told Jack. He told me you're approving everything that goes into the Sands, so I thought it best to let you know that there isn't anything I wouldn't do to have the honor of putting my curtain rods into the house that Frank built. Of course, curtain rods have gotten a raw public relations deal ever since the Kennedy assassination

Remember, Frank, when the Warren Commission was taking testimony for their report, and Oswald's friend, the guy that drove him to work that day, asked him what was wrapped in that blanket he was bringing with him to work? Oswald said, "curtain rods." Of all the professions in the world, this nut had to pick my product. It's a good thing he didn't say, "Some curtain rods made by Weiss & Rifkind—they're the only kind I hang in my home." I would be persona au gratin in this town, Frank.

Tomorrow I'm supposed to meet Doc Stacher in his office on the eleventh floor. I know he's like a father to you, Frank. I hope he turns out to be like an uncle to me. I know what you're thinking, Frank, "Be careful, Finkie, I know how to handle these guys. You don't."

Well, I checked up on the good doctor and, Frank, a little

atrocious assault, some larceny, and a hijacking charge that had no basis in fact doesn't scare old Finky. A guy's gotta make a living and that's that. Nathan Pitzler, Al Capone's favorite attorney, was an honored guest at my nephew Stewart's bar mitzvah. It will be an honor to meet the man who built the Sands. We're two Jews meeting in the desert to make a business deal, what could be so terrible?

The first night I got here, Frank, I made a pilgrimage to your suite on the ground floor. Very few people know how close you are to them while they're losing their shirts in the casino— you're on the ground floor in that three-bedroom suite the boys made for you. I knew you weren't in town, but I felt like paying homage. I thought I heard someone splashing around in the private pool beyond the stone wall, but I couldn't be sure. One thing was certain—the prosciutto and provolone were being flown in that night, because while I was saluting you with Jack Daniel's, a delivery was being made. The lights from the swimming pool made the prosciutto look like a piece of marble being carried to a pedestal in the Louvre. I knew then that you were on your way, although the next morning, I heard it was Jilly who was coming through town.

Jilly walks the earth for you, Francis. He makes the crooked places straight for you. He can shake a man's hand and know immediately if it's someone you should meet. He feels the bumps in the floor so you'll know where to walk. It's like the guy is a walking stethoscope.

Our world is changing, Frank. No one gets drunk anymore—

they get stoned. People make fun of the president. Some cartoon showed Johnson showing off his appendectomy scar, only it was in the shape of Vietnam. Ava Gardner has turned into Twiggy. Twiggy? She's built like a window-shade roller. Even Jean Nidetch—she's the founder of Weight Watchers, Francis—thinks that Twiggy is an unhealthy influence.

Jill used to go to Weight Watchers. She was in the first Weight Watchers class run by Nidetch herself. Jill wasn't even that heavy but she thought it would be a good way to meet the women in town. I think Jean Nidetch is a genius, Frank. I'm not sure carrying a small postal scale around with you to restaurants is the secret to a long and happy life, but waiting for Jill outside Nidetch's home every week made me think a lot about marriage.

I'm a lot like you, Francis, I couldn't marry anyone in show business. At first, I thought you were tough on Juliet Prowse, maybe too tough. But she did change her mind about going on with her career. What is it you said when she called to tell you the happy news that she was willing to hang up her tights and marry you? "Forget it, baby"? Juliet was some woman, Frank. I always used to get her mixed up with Abby Dalton, the actress who plays Joey Bishop's wife on his television show, but now that I have them straightened out in my mind, it's hard to believe you didn't weaken in your resolve. She reminds me of those photographs you used to see after the Second World War of Paris whores waiting in an empty street. She has the kind of face that just makes you think of big mirrors and a crooked lampshade marooned on a nightstand. I hope that doesn't embarrass you, Francis. I'm just admitting that there are such things for us to think about in this day and age when a man can't wear a hat anymore on the street.

Your pal,

Finkie

GLAD TO BE UNHAPPY

Dear Frank,

Today the mirror told me something I've secretly known about for some time. I'm not a kid anymore. Sure, I've known the world was changing. You can feel it in the air, like those storms that seem to come out of nowhere and turn some poor shmuck standing at the eighteenth hole into a lightning rod. It seems to be getting closer all the time. But it's an inescapable fact, Francis, that this April, old Fink'll be standing on the other side of fifty. I know that's a milestone around your neck, too, Frank.

I'm not a vain type of guy, Frank, but I sure don't hear the cheers of millions of guys anymore, like I did in the olden days when I was Lieutenant Finkelstein and respect seemed to stick to us like we were made out of magnets. Every night, wherever we went, it was like opening night. Every cigarette lighter worked, every drink stood neatly at attention. I remember taking Jill to the Copa, and the small lamp in the middle of the table made Jill's hair look like some outstanding gift, which I know I didn't deserve. I felt like everyone was looking at us differently because of her.

The other day, Frank, this guy uses a word, "fulminate," then after he uses it, he asks me if I knew what it meant. There were other people around—could you imagine this putz, Frank, trying to make me look foolish in front of Rosalie, this woman I've been seeing lately, a dead ringer, Frank, for Rita Moreno? So I tell this schmuck that of course I know what "fulminate" means. But then I have to leave the club and run like a maniac over to Doubleday, because I know they stay open late, and look the word up in the dictionary, then take the cab back to the club, sit down at the table, making excuses why I took so long in the john, and then about an hour after he first asked me, I tell the guy "to issue a thunderous verbal attack or demonstration."

Everyone at the table, including Rosalie, looks at me as if I've just suffered a stroke. "Fulminate," I said, "You asked me if I knew what it meant. That's what it means." I had a feeling that this guy didn't even remember asking me if I knew what "fulminate" meant, he was on to a new word, "copious," telling us that he didn't want any dinner because he ate "copiously" before going out. Thank God he didn't ask me what "copious" meant as I was running low on cab fare and wanted to drop Rosalie off before going on my way.

I think, Frank, Bennett Cerf is a good influence on you. I hear you're building up a pretty impressive library in the house. Like me, pal, you're hittin' the dictionary every night to improve your vocabulary. That will certainly have a "salutary" effect on your social standing, Mr. Sinatra. They say you're even beginning to collect art, and read art books. So when you say Tintoretto, I won't think its Sam Giancana's driver.

Jill's brother Joey was something of an artist, Frank. He even went to Paris on the G.I. bill and studied at the Beaux Arts. But Jill's parents put the kabosh on Joe's dream of becoming a painter. They told him how much they needed him in their fur business, and how artists all end up like in *The Tales of Hoffmann*, sitting up in bed with an umbrella to keep the roof from leaking on them. Well, little Joey did what he was told. Even though he came back from Paris, I swear Frank, with some wonderful paintings rolled up under his arm. A blue nun, standing in a courtyard. The orange rooftops outside his window in the Latin quarter (not our Latin Quarter). His landlady, asleep, naked on her couch. No wonder he never needed any rent money from home.

But the paintings wound up in our garage. After Joe died, I went out and had them all framed. It was the first time I saw Jill cry. She didn't cry during the whole time our marriage was falling apart, but seeing those paintings brought on Niagara Falls. Slowly I turn, step by step, inch by inch. . .

Joe did leave the fur business, with its minks hanging in the window like the salamis in Katz's. Remember "Send a Salami to Your Boy in the Army," Frank? The House of Bronstein was on 32nd Street, Francis. I used to visit Jill there, during the heavy season, when she would work for her father in the showroom. Joe wound up designing lipstick displays for Revlon. I know what you're thinking, Frank, but no, I don't think Jill's brother was a

little light in the loafers. In fact, he once had a date with Ingrid
Bergman.

To be truthful, Francis, he won the date in a raffle held by
his Air Force Squadron up in Alaska just before the end of the
war. I even saved a picture of Joey and Ingrid, surrounded by all
the boys in Joe's squad, who look genuinely happy for him. I
always wanted to ask what he and Ingrid talked about, trudging
through the snow on their way to a movie held in one of the bar-
racks.

I don't know why, Frank. I know the world was on fire
then, but it seems now like it was some golden age. I miss the
war in the way that I imagine a doctor misses the flu season,
or in the way Dempsey misses the ring. That's not saying the
war was a piece of cake, Frank. Even in the Special Services
Unit—I was a kind of impresario, bringing Joe Lewis in to box
in an exhibition—we had our troubles. Did I ever tell you that
Buddy Rich was in my unit, Frank? Yes, your old pal from the
Dorsey band. We were the only Jews in our platoon. Buddy
was pretty fierce back then. We had a real redneck captain,
he was a kid really, from Georgia, who kept asking us (in all
seriousness, Frank) to show him our horns. He said back
home they told him that "real Jews" had horns or little knobs
on their heads "like in the Bible stories," and he wanted to see
ours. Well, Buddy just got fed up with having to listen to all
this crap, and not just from Captain Method.(That was his
name. L.D. Method, from Decatur, Georgia.) We got grief
from the entire platoon, Frank, about what lousy fighters the

Jews are and how the Jews are to blame for getting us into the war in the first place, and how they control all the newspapers and the banks and that that's the reason we're all going to get ourselves killed, so that the Jews can keep making money. It was impossible to reason with these dumb kids, Frank. But Buddy, he wasn't going to take their shit. He became a judo instructor and the best rifleman in the whole camp. They never sent Buddy overseas either, Frank, because like me with Myron, he was classified 3-A, the only bread winner in the family.

Buddy and I lost our baby-fat in the war. We came back looking like prominent men. We didn't have to say anything to be heard. You could pick us out of a crowd. The ones who went, I mean.

Only once in a while (in boot camp mostly) did I ever hear Buddy grunt and say, "Frank should be here, goddamit to hell." I know that some people thought that's why all the girls fell for you during the war, that because you didn't join up, you had them all to yourself. Some of the guys resented it, they felt like you were over at the Paramount making time with their girls, when you should've been on Paris Island eating grass with the rest of us. I know for a fact, that DiMag signed up and Hank Greenberg, he must've been the other Jew in the army that we heard about. And I know that Tami Mauriello wore the uniform, because I got him into an exhibition match with Louis who must've not liked Tami much because he almost took the poor wop's head off. I know that half the Dorsey band joined the marines and that Glenn Miller was telling the air force band to take it nice 'n easy.

So when we all heard about how that hole in your eardrum was going to keep you out of uniform, I didn't curse you, Frank. I just wanted some of your luck to rub off on our platoon if we got sent over, which of course we didn't, which I guess was a kind of luck, but not the kind of luck you can enjoy with a clear conscience.

Nostalgically yours,

Fink

Dear Frank,

I hate it when I get this way. The sentimental side of my drinking. I even start feeling sorry for Myron. Did I tell you, Frank, my brother was picked up for indecent exposure outside a tennis court at Fire Island? Apparently Myron, who's got a secret life with his money, and has always been too cheap to buy himself privileges at the Fire Island Tennis Club, decided to change out of his tennis shorts and into a pair of slacks outside the locker rooms, when a cop saw him taking a leak near the cabanas and canasta tables. He arrested Myron for indecent exposure.

My brother only worked for a few years his whole life. After Jill read me the riot act about Myron, "It's either him or me," she said, I gave him our old Chevy and a thousand dollars and told him to go find a job. He thanked me by complaining that it wasn't enough money and that I had no idea how devastated he felt about our losing our parents at such an early age. I thought it was a cheap shot, Frank, to call up the Finkelsteins like that from the vastly deep. In fact, after I kicked him out of the house, so to speak, his asthma seemed to disappear, and he got himself a job as an insurance investigator.

This was the perfect job for my brother, the man of a thousand questions, each one more tedious than the next. By the time you get finished with Myron, you feel like you've cheated on your taxes, raped your wife and just lost all your money at the track. Yet, I don't know a thing about Myron's private life, who his friends are, if he's ever had a woman. He has a regular group of "boys" he plays poker with on Friday nights, and a few of them spend a couple of weeks on Fire Island during the summer. Myron says Fire Island is changing, that it's being taken over by conventions of interior decorators and men who like to pick out furniture together. So that he and his "acquaintances"—you can never call them friends, Frank, Myron doesn't want anyone to think he has friends, he calls them "acquaintances"—might move their moveable feast to the Concord up in Kiamesha Lake, in the Catskills.

But after about ten years as an investigator, Myron quit the insurance company and retired. He still lives in the same one room apartment in Washington Heights that we lived in after our parents died and we were old enough to be on our own. It depresses me to visit him there, and the Heights are becoming pretty dangerous. Myron's neighbor was just mugged in the lobby of the building. An elderly woman, they threw her down on the ground and started beating her with her own groceries before someone called the police.

Jill, who never got along with my brother, always wondered how he could afford to retire after just ten years as an insurance investigator. Jill thinks Myron took a bribe of some kind. One of his friends, a lawyer named Dave Day, gave Myron a new car as a gift for bringing some clients his way. I never thought about it before, but maybe she's right.

Myron and his friends spent one winter in Miami and ended up as extras on a movie being shot on Collins Avenue. It's funny, Frank, because Myron hates booze, never smokes (he calls it a "filthy habit") and never fails to give me a dirty look whenever I light up or take a drink. He always makes a big production of coughing, in a big theatrical sort of way, when we're in the car together and I start to smoke, rolling down the window so quickly you'd think the car was on fire. Anyway, I got a big kick out of hearing about Myron's work as an extra in of all things a nightclub scene, where he had to smoke about 400 cigarettes and pretend to have liquor in him all night. He couldn't resist the pay and free food, so I expected him to put up with the indignity of doing what we like to do for fun.

I must say, on Myron's behalf, that he's one loyal S.O.B., at least to me. I know I can call on him in a crisis, and he'll open up his mysterious checkbook for me if I need it. But I hate to see him living in that one room apartment we shared as kids. I hate to see him get so sentimental on Christmas—as if it's some holiday we all celebrated together in the shtetl. The guy just likes to make himself feel miserable and then to spread it around. He's still a great looking guy and it kills me to think that he still spends nights weeping because we lost so much when we were kids.

You're lucky, Frank, as an only child you didn't have to worry about who in the family was less than enchanted with you. If you happened to be sitting at Ciro's with someone who was working the room kind of sullenly, you could just get rid of them with a wave of the hand. But I can't do that, Frank, not without thinking, "Fink, you're the lousiest guy that ever lived."

Wishing you everything but brotherly love, brother,

I'm your pal,

Finkie

Dear Frank,

I just spent the night with Gypsy Rose Lee—although not the way you think, or the way I always dreamed it would happen. I was on my way home when I found myself snowed in at O'Hare airport in Chi. I was waiting it out in the TWA lounge which always reminds me of home, with its wood paneling and big bar, its television set and the posters of warmer destinations. When all of a sudden an amazingly handsome woman with a full body and exciting red hair starts up a conversation about how being stranded like this reminds her of working for Minsky and being on the Keith-Albee circuit. . . . Her boast was that she had been just about everywhere, done everything and knew everyone worth knowing. I felt like one of the boys in the front row cheering her on. But who is this woman, I thought to myself. I knew she was famous in the old nightclub days, and then it struck me like a gong, Frank. It's Gypsy Rose Lee for Godsakes. And she was trying to pick me up in the TWA bar.

She suggested that we get into a taxicab and go over to the Pump Room or the Chez Paree and "make ourselves useful." So I did, Frank. We took a Yellow Cab through the freshly falling snow right into the city and had dinner at the Palmer House. The maitre d' recognized Gypsy immediately, and gave us the best in the house (notwithstanding the fact that the restaurant was completely empty, as the snowfall was about to break a record, even for Chi). So imagine my delight to be sitting with the greatest ecdysiast in history, Frank, sharing an intimate dinner in the empty Palmer House with Gypsy Rose Lee as the waiters and busboys stood together like a choir in the corner of the room, waiting for our signal.

Gypsy told me how she retired at the age of forty-three, how a friend suggested she invest some of her money in the Arizona real estate market, and that now she was rich. She didn't even know how rich. She was very proud of having written a book, a murder mystery that takes place in a burlesque house, called *The G-String Murders*. She said she wrote it about twenty years ago, with the help of a guy named A-U-D-E-N, who called himself a poet and lived for a while with Gypsy in a big house in Brooklyn Heights. I didn't get the feeling that anything went on between them, but she sounded crazy about this guy, and called him a genius. She made a big deal of spelling out his name for me because she said most people couldn't pronounce it properly.

She had a lot of great stories, Frank, stories about Dolly Baxter, a stripper who even back in Gypsy's day was somewhat past her prime. She told me things about Stachi, the doorman at the Mocambo, and Hermit who got rid of the flies at El Morrocco, and we discovered that we had Sam Wing in common, the Chinese waiter who worked at Patsy D'Amore's place.

The problem was, Frank, I didn't know how far this thing was gonna go. Did she want to take a cab back to the airport? Was she going to take a room upstairs and wait in the city for the storm to pass? I was a little out of practice here, Francis. I still had Jill on the brain, and Rosalie, back home. But this was Gypsy Rose Lee, after all. Of course most women known for their rough wit and who have a lot of style make me a little anxious in the bedroom. It takes me a couple of nights to get used to them. I've had girls say I was the greatest in the sack they've ever seen, but not usually on the first night

So at the risk of being one of those sensitive types, I decided to tell this to Gypsy and how maybe just in the beginning, tonight anyway, maybe we should spend the night talking about you, Frank, and your fiftieth birthday party and keep reminiscing. Well, I must've looked like I had an apology painted on my face because Rose's giant eyes seemed to fill up with sympathy and she held my hand and she looked like she was going to start crying or something. She told me how romantic this evening was, and how she found me to be "a very attractive fellow," but she told me, Frank, that she was undergoing treatment for a woman's cancer and that in fact her hair isn't red at all, she was wearing a wig. Her doctors told her she had a pretty good chance of beating the Big C. Then she took my hand, Frank, and kissed it. She even gave me an autographed copy of her book, although I was too shy to read the inscription right in front of her. Later, on the plane going back to LaGuardia, I looked at it, "To Finkie—My Prince in the Snow. Love, Rose." You can't ask for better billing than that, right, Francis?

Finkie

Dear Frank,

Is it all right to miss your wife? I know you still get tears in your eyes for Ava as I get them in mine for Jill. I can still hear her little voice, thin but true, singing along to "No One Cares," and almost everything on *Only the Lonely*.

I guess all this started when a friend of mine, I guess he meant well, sent me an old newspaper clipping he found while cleaning out his desk. It looked to be from the *Daily News*, dated December 3, 1954. It was a picture of Jill and four other gals swooning and holding a sign that said: "Frankie Boy Is the Most—The Sinatra Swooners, Trenton N.J." I remember the day that picture appeared in the paper, Frank. It was ironic that Jill was in the newspaper as a Sinatra Swooner because she really didn't feel as strongly as I do about things Sinatra. In fact, that was one of the problems in our marriage. I remember though, how long she waited to get in to see you. It must've been at the Paramount Theater. *Suddenly* had just opened. It's funny when you consider how patriotic you are, Frank, that you got to play in two movies about Presidential assassinations. That's just one of the mysteries of show business, Frank, like the time when Jill and I happened to be in Chicago and were desperate for some entertainment, and the only thing we could get tickets to was a play called *Remains to Be Seen* with Tommy Sands, who at the time was married to Nancy Jr. We had just missed seeing you, Frank. I think we heard later that you were down to see your son in-law for his opening night.

I sometimes wonder if you started hating Tommy Sands after Nancy's divorce, or if you simply hate him by never thinking about him. As for me, I can't stop thinking not only about the people I hate, but the people I love. That's a funny way to go through life, isn't it Frank?

Jill and I tried to get back together once. But it was a disaster from the get-go. I thought I knew something about women, Francis. You don't spend four years in the army and not learn something about mice and their ways, but as much as we learn they seem to know that much more. It's just an optimum illusion that we're gaining on them, Frank.

Maybe the problem really got started when I began calling her Lulu—instead of, you should excuse the expression, her Christian name, Jill. I think it was because she looked so much

like Louise Brooks, that silent screen actress with the bangs—
they used to call her the girl in the black helmet—because her
haircut looked like an old Roman centurion's helmet. Louise
Brooks retired from the movies and wound up working in Macy's
at the cosmetics counter. I even had a picture of our Miss
Brooks in the movie *Pandora's Box*—where she played the part
of Lulu—taped to the inside of my locker at the Yacht Club.

Yes, Frank, the Yacht Club. I felt like Pal Joey, on Rita
Hayworth's yacht in that place, but Lulu's—Jill's—old man gave
it to us as some kind of wedding present. He vouched for us in
other words. And so they offered us a membership. It's like
Hillcrest in Beverly Hills. They kept all the Jews out of the boat-
ing clubs here, so they started their own. It became so exclusive
that even the Gentiles wanted to get in. I never even figured out
how the place worked. That first year we owed almost a thousand dollars to the club treasury. I thought all the phone privileges, quote unquote, were gratis, as well as the endless rum and
cokes we inhaled all summer long.

When I first met her, I was worried about Jill's spending
habits. I knew she came from dough. Her father had sold his fur
business to the Goodyear tire company for a bundle and I knew
how many window shades I'd have to sell to keep up with her.
Of course, Frank, I wanted to give Jill everything. I wanted to be
a lavish spender. First, because Jill looked so good in clothes and
second, because I wanted her old man to know I could do it.
"I'm gifting today," I would say, and take Jill by the hand and
bring her into the bedroom where a Chanel suit would be laid

out on the bed as if Jackie Kennedy had just been taking a nap there. Right beside a powder blue nightgown that reminded me what a pleasure marriage could be.

She always claimed that blue was her color and so one day, I took her out for the longest lunch in recorded history, while I had the whole house painted her color. But she became sore at me, Frank, for spending money in this way. You see, I learned something about the rich while I was married to Jill. That is, they're not like everybody else. I heard it a lot growing up. The rich are just people like you and me, only they have money and all the problems that that brings. Well, Frank, money brands you for life. Marrying me, Jill knew we weren't going to be able to live like she did when she was the princess of the House of Bronstein, and to her credit, that was alright with her.

But it seems, Francis, that I was on probation the whole time I was Jill's husband. It was like one of those stories I used to read to Nancy Ava in her book of gods and goddesses, where the Gods propose a test for the mortal suitor in the hopes that he is worthy of the Goddess's hand.

Well, Frank, the Bronsteins were testing me, to see if I was mature enough to handle some of old man Bronstein's doe ray me. Was I able to manage my own finances and live within my means? "You can't have champagne tastes and a beer pocket book," one of the Bronsteins told me once. And all the time I'm thinking to myself, "What if you have beer tastes and a champagne pocket book?" which pretty much describes the entire Bronstein clan.

So all this time, Frank, I'm trying to emulate Jill's father and they've both got their eye on me to see how careful I can be so that daddy wouldn't feel uncomfortable about giving us 100,000 dollars on his 70th birthday. He should live a hundred and twenty years, but apparently, I didn't pass the test, and so the money was put into some special account that no one can touch until the Messiah comes and we all walk out of our graves.

The whole thing would've been just too funny if it wasn't so sad. It was as if the Three Stooges had decided to become the patron saints of my marriage to Jill. How come women hate the Stooges, Frank? I guess they can't stand all that chaos, the mess in the kitchen. I think men like them, and go on liking them, because the boys keep screwing up—at work and at home. They're always getting into these impossible situations where they have to keep up pretenses. Pretending they're college professors, doctors, or private eyes. That explains a lot of the men I know. They're afraid of screwing up, never sure they're doing the right thing. Every man thinks he's an impostor, Frank. Sometimes I think everyone has this trouble but you, Frank. Every guy I know has to watch his step. Every man I know wants to throw a lemon meringue pie in his hostess's face, at least once in his life. Or extract his boss's tooth with a string attached to a racehorse.

After I had gone back to living on my own again, Jill and I did try to get together. But she had gone back to her old life and found my place "a little drab." She had developed a real allergy not just to my place—but to my way of doing things. "It's

Frank's world," I would tell her, "we only live in it." "Your friend Frank wouldn't live like this," she would say.

You know you're in trouble, Frank, when words like "drab" start creeping into their vocabulary. That, and the fact that it had become almost impossible to keep up with Jill's changing opinion of my estranged in-laws. First, Jill's mother was an extremely superficial woman whose voice was a cross between Tallulah Bankhead and an Atlantic City seagull. She seemed to take enormous pleasure out of irritating what life there was out of Jill's old man. Then later, on the telephone with her mother, she was absolutely brilliant, Frank, commiserating with her about how impossible the old guy was. They would even make jokes about hiding his glycerin pills. It was a cruel side that I hadn't seen before, Frank. And it scared the hell out of me. Also, I didn't know whose side to be on. I had heard so many crazy things. So I wound up outmaneuvering myself to the point where I'm about to celebrate your fiftieth, Francis, by going to the opening of *Von Ryan's Express* and then maybe Danny's Hideaway with Rosalie, although that's another conversation.

Well, Frank, at the risk of sounding like the old man in the mountain, the way I see it, we all pretty much want the same things out of life, Only I figure that if you can find a way to make the other guy ask first, then they can't bite your head off if it never works out.

Happy Birthday, Frankie.

Your pal,

Finkie

Dear Frank,

The house Jill and I lived in is up for sale. I even snuck in the other night and spent the night there. Slept in my old bed, walked out on the patio and drank a whole pot of coffee the next morning. You would have thought, to see me there, Frank, that Jill and Nancy Ava were going to come downstairs and join me there any minute. Then I did something a little crazy. I called a few of our neighbors—the husbands—and invited them over for a steam bath. I put a steam room in the house, Frank, after I heard about you putting one into Cal-Neva. I even called the same contractor you used, the Pucci Brothers. The Puccis—the one who lived in Eastchester we called Pucci East. The other brother, who lived in Westchester, we called Pucci West.

The Puccis, of course, were very proud of the work they did for you at Cal-Neva, Frank, but they refused to reveal exactly how the private steam room at Cal-Neva worked, or what it looked like. You'd think they were hired to work on the Manhattan Project. That's how closely they guarded the plans. They were even reluctant to tell me how they proposed to build the steam room in our house, telling us that by the time they were finished, even Swifty Morgan could slice off twenty pounds in one of their saunas. (Swifty Morgan was an old friend of mine, Frank. I think he tried to introduce himself to you when Cal-Neva first opened. He's a millionaire tie-salesman who always hustles me for ties and jewelry of dubious value. He always claims that his jewelry's hot. I think Swifty is indebted to his imagination for his facts, Frank. But the boys get a kick out of thinking they're buying stolen merchandise from some fabulous house in Sands Point. We like to think that it came from the private stash of a great second story man with suave Cary Grant manners. With a nickname given to him by Interpol, like the Cat.)

As I was saying, Francis, none of our fine gentlemen from the New Rochelle Civic Estates Association—my goddamned neighbors for chrissake—cared to steam off with yours truly, so I called the Puccis—East and West—to come over and join me for a soak.

The Puccis are big boys, Frank. And the three of us could barely squeeze into the tiny steamroom, originally built for Jill and myself. But we sat there on three towels and talked about how you almost drowned in Hawaii, a few years back, and we wondered what became of the young guy who rescued you, I think his name was Brad. After the kid saved your life, I don't think he was ever heard from again. Pucci West says the kid married an heiress of the StarKist tuna fortune. Pucci East says you took care of the guy by making him a producer on some of your recent movies. I tell both Puccis, East and West, that there might be another reason we never hear about Frank's rescuer. Maybe there's a love/hate relationship here, I told the two gigantic and naked Pucci brothers, sweating in my empty house, and maybe you didn't want the kid around reminding him that he'd saved your life.

The empty house made me think of Jill and then for some reason of Jill's father and then my own. I thought the world of my old man, Frank, but I don't think I ever told him how much I loved him. Maybe, once, when he came home from the laundry business he ran with another guy, and they got into a big fight; my father took another punch in the nose and came home with his nose broken again. I think I might've said it then. But never when he got just three hours sleep a night in order to be at the dry cleaning plant before the sun came up. You would've thought that he was carrying the whole secret of D-Day around with him, that's how serious he looked for those few hours when he was home. I never told him then how much he meant to me.

I think, Frank, I did the same thing with Jill. Of course, now she's in my thoughts more than ever. Where before she was the source of all my worry and anxiety, thinking about her now brings me a kind of contentment. Unfortunately, I think about Jill even though I see Rosalie about once a week.

Rosalie is the reason why my life has a bit of James Bond in it now. I bet you didn't know your old friend Finky had a talent for intrigue, did you Francis?

When Rosalie confessed her love for me, Frank, I can't say it came as a surprise. A man can have a woman's intuition, too, Frank. Even in the dark of the El Mocambo, I could tell the difference between Jill and Rosalie. Tenderness was certainly never something Jill had to work at (but then again, she could turn on a dime and cost you your life—I never saw anyone who could create an argument faster than Jill). Rosalie had to learn tenderness, like someone learns shorthand or how to parallel park. It was difficult for her, I know. It was a struggle. Though not for her children, who had a much different kind of life. Rosalie had to drop out of high school to help raise her family after her father split with all the bread. When Rosalie married Geoffrey Haines, the landscape architect who designed all those golf courses down South, she found herself in a very different world. Her children all had telephones in their rooms with private numbers! They all wound up in private schools. Rosalie told me that once, when she got into a big fight with her daughter about staying out late, that in the middle of the argument her daughter corrected her mother's grammar. Apparently, Haines was away a lot and while the kids couldn't wait to see their father, Rosalie started to dread the reunions with her husband.

A friend of mine says that it's understandable, then, that Rosalie would begin to get restless, that she would turn to other men and finally, Frank, to me.

Sometimes I think Rosalie is making a pretty big mistake being with me, Frank. I wonder if the two of you might have crossed paths at some point? Did I tell you that she supported her family by dancing in places like the Latin Quarter and the Copa? That's where Geoffrey Haines first noticed her—he had just been hired by Bing Crosby, and I think Harry Rupp, to work on Pebble Beach. Rosalie told me that if I had been at the Copa that night, Francis, Haines wouldn't have stood a chance. It would've been a boat race.

Rosalie is not a neurotic woman, Francis. But she can act capriciously. (You don't have to look that one up, Frank, it means after you've done nothing but lavish attention on a chick for six months and all of a sudden she tells you you've been treating her like a pane of glass, looking right through her to the other side of the room and she locks you out of your house— that's capricious, Frank.) Still, I worry about her leaving me for a younger man. I'm at that dangerous age, Francis. My hair's turning gray, my handicap is somewhere near the Standard & Poor's index, and I've got eyeglasses in my eyeglasses, for reading. So my love for Rosalie is something so deep, Frank, that I can't bring myself to share it with her. It would be the ultimate compliment that I cannot make. But my quiet about all this has had a strange effect on Rosalie. She's become obsessed about my life with Jill, convinced that somehow we might be getting back together. She's eager to know all the details of our marriage. She wants to know if I ever "cheated" on Jill, especially during my trips overseas. She once asked me if Jill was the kind of woman who would question a man's virility when she got mad. Of course, I took a page out of your book, Frank, and refused to answer those kinds of questions. This only helped to make Rosalie even more upset, but I couldn't possibly tell her the truth and admit that at one time I did intend to remain married to Jill, and that I would have done anything to restore myself to her good graces but that I just didn't know how, or what it would take. Admitting that now, Frank, seemed almost vulgar, if not mean. So I took the fifth and said nothing.

Eventually, Rosalie gave up all this rutting around in the past. I was convinced that we had buried that bone of contention so deep that no one could ever find it. But Rosalie had hatched another plan, Frank, that was even worse. She wanted to meet Jill.

I thought this was about the craziest and most dangerous idea I ever heard. When Rosalie informed me that she didn't need my permission to meet Jill or anyone else for that matter, I backed down. I knew the more I objected, the more determined she would be to find Jill and take her out for the lunch from which no good could come. She might even show up at the club, in the middle of the Bronstein bridge game, which would be the end of my reputation as we know it. Or at the very least, Francis, endanger the rapprochement I have going with the Bronsteins—who after all are Nancy Ava's grandparents, and still very interested in helping New York's neediest, which I'm hoping will include me, the father of their darling granddaughter.

As of this writing, Rosalie has cooled down. But that's what they said about Pompeii.

Your pal,

Fink

Dear Frank,

I ran into Soupy Sales at Jilly's the other night, Frank, and asked him to sign a napkin for Nancy Ava, who thinks he's a riot. I told Jilly how much I loved *September of My Years* and how it made me feel too old for Rosalie. Jilly, the wise philosopher, said that fifty wasn't old, and that since it was Rosalie who had fallen in love with me that we were in this thing together and that I should ignore all the old jokes about an aging man and a young woman. Jilly said that you don't even make jokes like that, Francis, since you met Mia.

Mia and her mother were at Arthur's the other night, that new discothéque that Richard Burton's wife just opened. When I saw a telephone being brought out to them on the busy dance floor I thought to myself, they've got to be taking a call from Frank. Who else could track down a young girl and her mother in the middle of a discothéque?

It wasn't my kind of scene, Frank, but Rosalie likes to see all the new dance crazes. Although I feel a little funny dancing that way. During something called the "mashed potato" I bumped into Hermione Gingold and Van Johnson—they were doing "the frug" together. It looked to me as if Van Johnson threw his back out and had to go sit down. I went over to apologize to him. He was very gracious and said this was really a young person's place. I said I agreed with him and he invited us to sit down and join him for a drink. Rosalie said it was one of the most exciting nights of her life. I used to think that a man's dignity was more important than his stamina. But that night at Arthur's, I wasn't sure I had either.

But you must know how I feel, Frank, if you feel the same way about Mia. I've built up such a powerful desire for her, Frank, that nothing in the past—even my life with Jill, my love for Nancy Ava—nothing can compare to it. When I heard that Mia was missing from your fiftieth birthday party, I felt terrible for you, but then I realized that if it was Nancy Sr., who gave you the party, then of course Mia's being there was out of the question. It's hard getting used to being happy, isn't it, Frank? You have to learn to do it—like learning to write with your right hand. I was never right-handed in anything I did, but at school, I remember spending an entire year learning to write with my right hand. Everyone in those days, Frank, thought it was the thing to do. Somehow it looked more dignified for a man to use his right hand that way. "What about Dizzy Dean?" I said, "What about Don Larsen? Don't they inspire confidence?" But I guess I should be grateful, Frank. They could've said, "There goes Lefty Finkelstein," and I probably would've been ruined for life. Only, occasionally when I see a genuine southpaw in action, signing his name on a Diner's Club receipt or throwing a few curve balls into his kid's glove, I catch myself staring in awe as if he was breaking an Olympic record or something. And I find myself thinking, Fink, you used to be able to do that— before they forced you live in the land of the right-handed men. And now if I touch Rosalie's face with just my left hand, I'm not sure I really feel anything at all. It's almost like a phantom limb by now. That's why I hold her face in both my hands like Montgomery Clift does Elizabeth Taylor's in A *Place in the Sun*.

I met Jill for lunch the other day, Frank, at a little place off Madison in the thirties called Bienvenue. Jill likes it there, seeing that we used to meet there for lunch in the golden age when Jill worked practically around the corner in her father's showroom and I would come uptown from Weiss & Rifkind. Those were the days when sometimes, Frank, neither of us would go back to work that day but sneak off to the Roosevelt Hotel and "our room" overlooking Grand Central Station.

Maybe that's how we should've kept things between us. But then of course, Nancy Ava probably wouldn't have made it into the picture. But I see in *Life* magazine how today kids are living together on communes, in teepees, it's like a kibbutz in Israel, for chrissakes. Nancy Ava would like to go one summer and stay with our relatives there. Perhaps you visited a kibbutz in Israel, Frank, when you went to make *Cast a Giant Shadow* there with Yul Brynner? There was a picture of you and Angie Dickinson visiting Bethlehem that one of the secretaries put on my desk. The trip to the Holy Land must have really affected you, Francis.

But to get back to my lunch with Jill. It was soon pretty clear that this would not be one of those lunches that would end up with our walking the streets of this old town as if we were the only lovers left in New York. No, Frank. Not after what Jill had to tell me.

"You should've been at my father's last night," she said, wasting very little time. "I had a visitor. A very pretty young woman. In fact, at first glance I thought she might be one of Nancy Ava's friends." I knew it was Rosalie, Frank. First off, just like you, I'm used to those kinds of jokes by now. And in the second place, I derived some secret satisfaction from the fact that

Jill was letting me know that she thought Rosalie was attractive. For me, Frank, that admission was a significant private victory. Because it was one of the early warning signs of Jill's growing anger toward me that she began to concentrate on the beauty flaws of other women, complete strangers—movie stars, waitresses, models on billboards. I always knew driving back home from the Catskills after a weekend visiting Jill's parents that I was in for it, even with Nancy Ava asleep in the backseat, when Jill began seeing signs on the New Jersey Turnpike for Camay beauty soap, and she would start in on how the model's nose was too big, or how could they use someone whose eyes were so far apart, or who had such big hands. Eventually, she would get around to what was really bothering her and it was usually something I had done, or more likely had failed to do.

Nancy usually slept through most of this, although occasionally she would wake up and tell us to stop "talking." I don't think she knew the word "arguing" back then.

I was furious with Rosalie for disobeying me. I pleaded with her not to try and visit Jill, that it couldn't possibly mean anything to her, that it was just morbid curiosity. Perhaps this is reminding you of that incident back in the fifties when you found Ava Gardner and Lana Turner in bed together, in *your* house. If memory serves me correctly, didn't you call the cops when you came home?

So I asked Jill for a rundown on what Rosalie wanted. Other than a look at the way I used to live. "From what I hear," Jill said, "I don't think Rosalie Haines needs to look at the

Bronstein House, not the way she used to live with Geoffrey Haines. In fact," she added, plunging the knife in a little deeper, "she claims you spent a little time there, as a guest of hers and her husband.'"

"But what did she want?" I practically pleaded with Jill to tell me something I didn't already know.

"She wanted to talk to me about becoming partners, opening a nightclub." If someone, Frank, had poured a cup of espresso down my pants at that moment, I don't think I would have been capable of so much as a twitch. "I hope you don't mind my saying this," Jill explained, "but I told your 'friend' that I got the feeling from talking to you that she was one of those people who gave opportunism a bad name, and that she wasn't really as interested in owning a nightclub as she was interested in owning you." Jill knew how to be polite if she wanted to be, Frank. She was just setting me up for a terrible scene with Rosalie, later that day or perhaps, even worse, the next day at the office. The fact that she allowed Rosalie to think there was any chance that Jill or the Bronsteins would back her cockamamie idea for a nightclub violated the Geneva Convention for the treatment of prisoners of war, which certainly describes Rosalie in the Bronstein house, Frank.

In the war between the Bronsteins and myself, Frank, Rosalie had simply wandered onto the battlefield.

The next day Rosalie appeared in my office just as I had predicted she would. Before even acknowledging her I looked down the hallway to see who else was around. Ten forty-five in the morning is the perfect time, Frank, for finding just about everyone at their desks. But the halls looked pretty empty and I figured that if Rosalie didn't raise her voice, there was a slim chance that the entire drapery hardware industry might not learn all the particulars of our relationship—after all, I had been in the habit of blaming myself for all of the problems Jill and I were having, which only succeeded in turning Jill into a saint in the eyes of everyone who worked that stretch of real estate on Fifth Avenue between Twenty-Third and Twenty-Seventh Streets, dominated by the Hornick Building.(The Hornick business is huge, Frank, but I wouldn't trade places with Harry Hornick for all the tea in China. Because then I would be married to Harry's wife, Lita Hornick, who I'm convinced is a female impersonator, who has been able to keep this a secret from Harry by running around to all the downtown art galleries, spending Harry's money on Andy Warhol paintings of Brillo boxes!)

Rosalie never raised her voice, but she parroted back all the half-truths that Jill had diabolically concocted to put the worst possible light on just about everything I had ever told her about Rosalie, which, Frank, you can be sure wasn't much as I still harbored (what I now know to have been) the ridiculous fantasy of one day getting back together with Jill. All I hoped for now was that Rosalie would leave as quietly as possible or at least tell me that her idea for a nightclub was simply an excuse to see if Jill still had any feelings left for me, which, as I contemplate it now, Frank, wasn't such a crazy thing for Rosalie to have done, when you consider that she never could get a straight answer out of me.

I sat pretty much in silence, Frank, as Rosalie heaped con-
tumelies (I ain't just readin' Earl Wilson, pal) on me and Jill.
"What a great partnership this'll be," I thought to myself, as
Rosalie became furious at me for the condescending way she felt
Jill and her family had treated her.

You see, Frank, that's why I'm playing *September of My
Years*, over and over again, until the hi-fi needle is a nub ground
into dust. "The Man in the Looking Glass" kills me and of
course, "September Song." It gives hope to us humans, at least
for one more night. But as much as I love it, it hurts to listen to
it. I realized that if something were to happen to you Frank, I
don't think I could listen to the records anymore—I couldn't—
at least not for a very long time.

Your Pal,

Finkie

Dear Frank,

After Rosalie pulled her stunt with Jill about the nightclub
and then came to my office to give me a tongue lashing, I knew
people in the building would be talking about us for weeks, the
way they can't seem to get enough about you and the Butterfly
(isn't that what that guy with the long mustache that goes up
like knitting needles—Dali—isn't that his nickname for Mia?).

Usually, I have lunch in the coffee shop on the ground floor
of the Hornick Building. It was a couple of weeks before anyone
asked me about Rosalie and her visit to the office. But it was

only after I was away for a couple of days, Frank, that I began to notice the awkward looks and uncomfortable silences and I realized that people really were talking about me. You probably don't even notice this anymore, Frank. But this kind of attention is new to me.

The first person to say anything about it to my face was Arthur Berkel, a vice president of Kirsch Hardware, a competitor but a life-long friend. "Finkie," he said, "you can tell me if I'm out of line here, but are you in any kind of trouble, I mean if there's anything I can do. . . ?"

"Arthur, I've never lied to you. So I'm not going to start now. I don't know exactly what the talk on the street is but I'm sure that even Smokey the Bear couldn't put it out now."

"Well," Arthur said, "it's certainly not as bad as Larry Silverberg." That, Frank, was a reference to a story that had become almost a kind of legend in the drapery hardware business, and one of the most famous stories on the strip (which meant the showrooms around 28th Street, which really meant the Hornick Building and its satellites).

Larry Silverberg was a bad egg, Francis. A buyer for May's department stores who was always pestering reps for theater passes, Yankee tickets, that sort of thing. Everyone in the business knew about this guy and hated his guts, but May's is a gorilla of an account, Frank. And it's not worth losing over a couple of lousy baseball games. So most of the reps I knew paid Silverberg at least something on the side, in exchange for a big order.

But Silverberg was not a gracious crook, Frank. Usually, after he made his load and agreed to do business with you, he would make some sarcastic personal remark which you were powerless to do anything about. If, like me, you hemmed and hawed about forking over thirty-five dollars a week to the Larry Silverberg Foundation, he would find out where you lived, and knew when to visit you at home. I remember once, Frank, when Silverberg appeared on my driveway with a bouquet of roses for Jill and a little satchel of chocolate coins for Nancy Ava. So the guy was smart, Frank. He quickly got all the ladies on his side. Criticizing Larry Silverberg was like trying to find someone to say something bad about the Pope. He played every side of the street. He had it covered, that is until he met Anita.

Anita was a beautiful Negro from Barbados Larry had hired as his assistant. Before too long the two of them were taking their lunch breaks at a Holiday Inn near the Westchester Shopping Center. Anita really was a stunning woman, Frank. She looked a lot like Lena Horne. Larry was married of course and had two kids. In fact, he lived near us in New Rochelle. His oldest girl and Nancy Ava were in junior high together. It was on Washington's birthday last year that Anita shot Larry Silverberg and then took her own life in a heart-shaped bathtub in the Poconos, where Larry and Anita had begun to go on weekends.

Whenever I'd go for a walk in the neighborhood, I always avoided the Silverberg residence, afraid I'd run into his wife and kids. The old me was quite a coward, Frank. I felt sorry for them, that Larry put them through all that.

Most of the big shots I know are dead, Frank. But none of them ever got shot, not even in the war. Only a little guy, one of the small fry, whose recklessness got him killed.

So needless to say, Frank, I was relieved when Arthur gave me that compliment with his right hand, that Rosalie's temper tantrum, while newsworthy, didn't create half the stir Larry Silverberg's untimely demise did.

It's not easy, Francis, to talk about all this to you, particularly now when you seem so happy like a man in love. You'd have to be in love to spend 85 G's on an engagement ring, Frank. I'm sure you made the folks at Rusar's Jewelry very happy. I managed to pick up one of those engraved cigarette boxes you had made for all the performers at the Kennedy Inaugural Ball. It was incredibly generous of you, Frank, to allow Rusar's to engrave it—"To Finkie, who wasn't there. January 20, 1961." I will always treasure it. It's the first thing I told Jill she wouldn't be able to touch in the divorce.

In the old days, Frank, if Rosalie had come to my office spewing such hateful things, I would have lashed back, fought the good fight, defended myself from this kamikaze attack on our relationship. But instead, Frank, I listened in silence, a complete blackout. You would've thought I was one of the Mercury astronauts during the re-entry phase, when Cape Canaveral loses all contact with the capsule, until it re-enters the earth's atmosphere, until you can practically see it coming over the horizon.

But something happened to me, Frank, in the office that day. It was like I was celebrating a birthday or something. The birthday of a new Finkie. The old Finkie, the old me is telling you the story about the new me, the one who listened quietly while Rosalie railed at the old me in the office. I know what you're thinking, Francis, "Finkie's flipped his lid. That book-of-the-month club jazz is finally getting to him." But the truth is, Frank, that of course the old me and the new me are essentially the same Fink. We carry around the same name, the signature on the back of the Diner's Club card is still the same, we sit in the same place in the synagogue during the high holy days and yet, Frank, no one really knew at exactly what precise moment the old me became the new me. Of course, Frank, when Dean played the Copa in New York, and all the busboys greeted Rosalie and me like they were our long lost sons, it was all happening to the outer me, the me that everyone sees, but, Francis, it was the inner me, the new me that Rosalie was talking to at 10:45 A.M. in the Hornick building. The one who refused to get down in the mud with her. Who, if the truth be known, still wants to be with her again.

I'm pretty certain, Frank, that no one really knows what went on between Rosalie, Jill and myself. And if they do know, well, the new me doesn't care in quite the same way. The old Finkie wanted Rosalie, wanted her to be my wife, but the old Finkie was trapped—he couldn't shake off the idea that Jill and I belonged together. But what was really transpiring, Frank, was that the old me was simply too much of a coward to tell Rosalie how I felt and therefore kept Jill around as a kind of "bond" on an exciting woman, Frank, and so unlike anyone he had ever known, that arguing with her was like a kind of electric shock for Haines—as the headshrinkers like to say, it was a catharsis for him, Frank. A catharsis of joy.

It's safe to say, Frank, that Rosalie was a flop as a conventional wife. But who wants a conventional wife, right Frank? But as we both know, unconventional wives have a way of asserting themselves. At first, Rosalie amused her husband. But before too long he started to feel the way you must've felt with the Barefoot Contessa, that he was living alongside some exotic and highly-strung animal. Eventually, this got to be too much for Haines, and that, along with his incessant traveling, certainly helped to put the kabosh on the kind of relationship that they had both been looking for. It was at that point, Frank, at which I made my entrance.

Now, Frank, I suppose I was something of a shadowy figure to Geoffrey Haines, because remember, Rosalie was only separated from him when we first started seeing one another. I met him once when Rosalie had the brilliant idea to have me pick her up at the Westchester Golf and Country Club.

You'll probably relate to this, Frank, when you hear that Geoffrey Haines had a reputation that many of his associates in landscape architecture called "volatile," as in "He's a volatile personality." To me, Frank, that word was always Greek for "son-of-a-bitch." But that was all before I ever met him. I never really doubted for a minute that the guy didn't know who the hell I was. I mean, it's been my experience, Frank, that these country club types are as fond of gossip as my grandmother's sewing circle. But Haines said nothing when I met him. He simply pumped my hand once or twice and then just let me take his wife away in my car. I do remember the way he looked at me though, it was as if he was handing over a dangerous prisoner to the authorities. I wouldn't exactly call it a smile but a kind of grin like you see on a butler's face in the movies when he knows the guest is about to walk through the wrong door into a closet, or worse, into his master's bedroom.

I guess Rosalie was closest to her sister, Frank. In fact, the last time I saw Rosalie, her sister was there. I don't think Rosalie's sister ever really liked me. For one thing, she hated men. She was married to a little guy she liked to boss around by the name of Georgie. She was built like Rosalind Russell and protected Rosalie even when Rosalie wasn't in any kind of danger. The last time I saw Rosalie her sister was there in the apartment while Georgie sat outside in the car, waiting. I noticed him sitting in front of the apartment when I went up. So I knew what to expect. I just stared at the brass plate on the floor of the elevator—the word Otis—I thought of standing inside the "O" with Rosalie and her sister, while Georgie held the "t" like a cross just outside the circle. I had all sorts of crazy thoughts like that going up to Rosalie's apartment. Both women were waiting for me, Francis, in the living room. The whole thing looked pretty well rehearsed to me. "I didn't think we needed a chaperone at our age," I told Rosalie. I remember making some tasteless remark about how I don't swing with my girlfriend's sister in the same room, unless of course she had other ideas. But these girls were beyond being shocked, or amused by anything I might've said, Frank.

So I asked Rosalie if she was afraid of being alone with me, and she told me that it was only natural for her sister to keep her from becoming too emotional at a time like this. To protect her from being intimidated by me. That was the word she used, Frank, "intimidated," as if I was some hood that had come to "talk" to her about an I.O.U.

"Are you scared of me, Rosalie? Do you think I'm going to hurt you, you silly nut?" I guess you could say that was my parting shot, Frank. I'm not much for staircase wit, Francis. Not very effective, I grant you, but at the time it was the best I could do.

I never saw Rosalie again, Frank. What I know about her I read in the newspapers, about her going back to Geoffrey Haines, and relocating to Florida, Ft. Lauderdale, I believe.

Someone told me, Frank, that when you finally married your Mia, "Strangers in the Night" was playing softly throughout the hotel. I heard it was 107 degrees in Vegas that day.

After I walked out of Rosalie's apartment and leaned in Georgie's window to tease him about the lousy parking job, I got back in the car, put on the radio and what do you think I heard? "Strangers in the Night," quite a song for a man on trial to hear, because if ever a man was on trial, Frank, it was me.

Your pal,

Finkie

STRANGERS IN THE NIGHT

Dear Frank,

How wrong can a guy get? When I read that the Butterfly and your lawyer Mickey Rudin were in Nicaragua, I knew it couldn't be good news. Nicaragua, Frank? Did you see how they stoned Bobby Kennedy when he went down there? Not that you'd be upset about that, not after what Bobby's put you through, Francis.

I had high hopes for you and Mia. You guys lasted about as long as Rosalie and yours truly, a year and a half. I remember the time just before Rosalie and I started to see one another almost every day—it was April, my birthday—and it was spring, of course. It's funny how some women don't exist for us in the winter, Frank. The spring is when the whole ball of wax seems to take shape. That's when my feelings for Rosalie seemed to come into being. A friend of mine says that the spring is when all those old romantic movies start to play themselves out in your mind—though they never get made in real life.

I decided to confide in Myron, of all people, with talk about Rosalie, Jill and that whole boatload of sensitive bullshit about having only one true love, and knowing when she's right there, standing in the same room with you. Recognizing that, Frank, that's the hard part. It's hard to love in the present tense, isn't it, Francis? I know that as soon as I met Rosalie I started to live in the future. I told Myron how practically immediately after making love to Rosalie for the first time, I proposed going on a trip to Europe. "You'll see April in Paris," I told her. But she was smarter than me, Frank. She knew that the future was just another trap I had set for myself out there. "I'm not worried about what's going to happen six months from now," Rosalie would say, "Why should you?"

It's time for that empty feeling, again, Francis.

I remember thinking, just before you got married, that it's not going to be easy. After all, she's so young. But I thought to myself Fink, they've got to try. Maybe they'll only be able to have a couple of years together, but like Rosalie and me, it gave one the feeling that there was still some fruit left to life, even if as a great man once said "it's half way down the tree."

But if I know you, Frank, you're worried more about Mia than about yourself. Because that's how I felt, even after Rosalie and her sister watched me walk out of that apartment forever. When you get to be our age, Frank, you've already built a moat around yourself. You don't let yourself hurt as much as you used to.

Maybe in the end, age does matter. I used to dream about Rosalie becoming the happy genius of the Finkelstein household. But it was just a dream. And after all, Frank, a dream is a fantasy, and at the end of the day the fantasy is over and guys like us have to return to the real world. Rosalie, like Mia, they just wanted a friend, someone to guide them through the world. They really didn't want anything else from us. And, anyway, if Rosalie really wanted more than that from me, I probably couldn't have given it to her. I was off on my own island staring at the night to come. Even Jill, who really knew how to make with the words (after two years at a fancy sleep-away school in Illinois) used to say, "Fink, after ten years of marriage I'm still unable to fathom your complexities."

But maybe, in the end, Frank, everything that happens in love is for the best. You can't eat yourself up thinking about all these people, the Rona Barretts of the world, sitting around, waiting for the next break-up. They're squares, Francis, and the world is round. You just can't think about them.

Come to think of it, Frank, Jill always hated when I used that word. She hated "hipsters," as she called them. She said they all suffered from an "inferiority complex." She claimed that whenever we were out in public and a guy would pay her a compliment, I would "retaliate" as she put it, by calling him a square. Rosalie remembered one time when she told me about something nice her father had said about me, behind my back, and how I responded by telling her that "whatever her father was he definitely was not a square."

Jill and Rosalie and Mia are three women who possess dignity, Francis. For all of her youth, Mia seems like the kind of woman who, like Rosalie, maybe like all women, Frank, open themselves up to a veritable world of pity, and on that world, Frank, are oceans of compassion, and most of the women we know are drowned by it. Maybe this is the real problem, Frank, that women are better than we are. That first we make their world brutal and then ask them to live in it. Maybe that's why Jill asked me to leave our house, and Rosalie split and Mia went back to her mother. Maybe they just decide they can't stand to listen to our stories anymore. Maybe that's why Mia didn't want anything from you, and only took her stuffed animals from the bedroom, and the ring you gave her.

So here we are, bachelors again, Frank, wandering through the bottom of the world, just missing each other as we move through one saloon after another. Maybe that's why you can sing the way you do, Francis, your voice becoming even greater through the small storms and great alarms of your life and the lives of others, guys like me—we form a kind of chain of defeats, Frank, that lead back to you. And all that suffering turns up on a record, which we play more often than not in the dark to ourselves, or if we're "lucky," to one of those women who never really believed we ever loved them in the first place. Women who reach out for us in the private dark only to find a man thinking to himself about whether or not he should sell his car or mortgage the house. I once heard a guy compare marriage to the end of a vacation, Frank, when you are forced to face the seriousness of your life, and you have to think about starting from scratch, or at the very least, begin again the work you've been unable, or unwilling to do. To admit to yourself that what you've been feeling all those months and years were real. We thought we could avoid having to listen to that voice that told us to get closer to those we shared our life with. Sometimes, I admit it, I even turned the hi-fi up so that your voice would drown out that other voice I heard. But it never really worked that way.

It's like what I tried to explain to Myron, a guy who's never gotten close to anyone, about the pain of pain.

You know what that is, Frank? That's when after you've been kicked out of the house and you pull into a gas station to fill up the tank, to go God knows where, and you kick the front tire to see if it needs any air, and you kick it so hard that you practically break your foot, so that now you can really howl at the moon and bring tears to your eyes, that's the pain of pain, Frank. And so I hope there's an all night-service station on the road to Palm Springs, pal. I know I'll be happy to see you.

Finkie

Dear Frank,

I'm sure that with all you've been through—the divorce, your being over in England to make *Naked Runner*—you've just been too busy to get back in touch with old Fink, but as I've said before, Francis, you're still 10 inches taller than any guy I know.

We buried Uncle Dave last week. You remember Uncle Dave, Frank? He was the guy with the Mr. Clean haircut who lived out in Hollywood and was a bullwhip specialist. The last time I saw Uncle Dave was in New York. He had gotten a job in a Carol Channing musical where he was supposed to pull off Carol Channing's sequined gown with one crack of his bullwhip and then walk off while she tries to cover herself standing on-stage in her slip.

Dave never made it back to California after that, Frank. He stayed on to work for Earl Wilson at the *Post*. I don't think Uncle Dave was any more popular at the *Post* or at Earl Wilson's table than he was at Musso Frank's or on the lot at Paramount, but it was hard to get rid of him. You might be asking yourself, Frank, why did people put up with him? He wasn't a particularly generous or even friendly guy. He had an impossibly imperious air about him—if that's the right expression—he always used to go on about how he descended from the white Russians, and how in Hollywood he would never be kept waiting like in New York.

In the beginning we merely felt sorry for Uncle Dave, his whole Taras Bulba routine: the bald head and barrel chest, his hopeless name-dropping, and that absurd specialty of his which really belonged in the Moscow Circus and made the New York crowd treat him more like a clown than anything else. Later they would discover there was almost no way to get rid of Uncle Dave.

You see, Frank, Dave made his real living by selling "items" to the gossip columnists. Of course, the newspapers they worked for like the *Daily Mirror*, or the *Journal-American*, never wanted to acknowledge that guys like my Uncle Dave even existed. So they would always refuse to pay him for his information. Instead Dave had to rely on handouts from his competitors, small time press agents, who wanted to see their "clients'"

they lost their sense of direction, and had no place else to go.

One thing is certain, Frank. Making the rounds with Uncle Dave changed my mind about Broadway. I didn't see Damon Runyon or "Apple Annie," Frank. That's strictly for the out-of-towners, Frank. I know you played the proprietor of the oldest established permanent floating crap-game in New York. But *Guys and Dolls* I didn't see when I went out on the town with Dave Finkelstein.

The women who seemed to frequent Uncle Dave's table were not much better. And Uncle Dave always had a way, I'd call it a kind of genius, Frank, of being able to embarrass me around his female friends. Treating me like I was his country cousin, and then under his breath telling me which ones he had been to bed with, and which ones he intended to "give to me."

It took this writer friend of Uncle Dave's to point out to me, Frank, that whenever a small group of eight or nine customers wanted to sit together in a night club, and tried to extend the table in a booth by moving some of the furniture around with the help of a waiter who seemed to know most of them by name, including a few new faces who had just come into town, this writer noticed, Frank, that no one seemed to clear a place for Uncle Dave. And it was true, Frank. After it was pointed out to me, I can't say that I ever heard anyone ask Uncle Dave to sit down and enjoy the party.

After that, I really observed Uncle Dave, Frank, I started to watch him as if I was preparing a report for J. Edgar Hoover. But Dave's New York life wasn't all that different from the way he had lived in Hollywood. Living on hope with every breath. He was a bore and an awfully cheap guy, and just because he had exhausted everyone around him (they couldn't even be bothered to insult him, Frank), he had himself convinced that he had become an important man.

I soon got the feeling, Frank, that if Uncle Dave had taken a full-page ad in the Sunday *New York Times*, no one would have noticed it, least of all his fellow night crawlers.

Uncle Dave wouldn't like to hear this, Frank, but he was as stage-struck as a young girl. He wanted to be able to sit for his Sardi's caricature and to see his name mentioned in *Variety*. He would've been willing to live his whole life over again if just one person would have recognized him walking through the lobby of the Warwick Hotel. He wanted women like Virginia Cherril to put it in their appointment books, when he was coming back to the coast.

Uncle Dave had no business going into the movies, Frank, not with that heavy accent and without any real talent, except for his bullwhip. But he couldn't help himself. In fact, his lack of any material success only succeeded in making him even more obstinate about sticking around, putting up with all sorts of personal insults, and as I could see for myself, treated as a kind of leper, even by the other Jews on Broadway. It was a wonder to me that Dave was even able to place anything in the columns.

I started to think about Uncle Dave, at one point, like that man who became a Roman emperor, the one who stuttered and who everyone treated as a kind of idiot. His family acting so freely, so candidly in front of this man, treating him as if he wasn't even there, until he knew all their secrets and he became the most powerful Roman of them all. I remember Jill was reading a book about this guy, the year we busted up. But I'm afraid that Uncle Dave didn't become the emperor of Broadway, Frank, or the king of anything. Toward the end, he had a dream of moving to Arizona, and an even bigger dream of writing his memoirs like he was Ulysses S. Grant, or someone who had lived an incredible life, which when you think about it long enough, I guess he had. In fact, Frank, the most interesting part of Dave's life, his life in Russia just before the revolution as a young man conscripted into the Tsar's army, was the one thing you could never get him to talk about.

I used to tell him that his stories would make a great play, that he could be another Clifford Odets, if he'd put it all down on paper. "Then let Clifford Odets write it," he would say. Or else he would explain to me how if they made a motion picture based on his life he would make himself available as a technical advisor, or that possibly he could appear as a Cossack who uses a whip on the people of his Russian village. You would think, Frank, that that kind of part would make him sick, "But that's the show business," he would tell me, "You've got to be ready for anything."

There was one person who cared what happened to Uncle Dave, Frank. Her name was Carla Page and she was a secretary to the Broadway impresario Arthur Hopkins. She decoded

Hopkins's broken English and even was allowed the high honor and privilege of signing his checks. She called Katharine Hepburn "Kate" and had a pet name for Ronald Coleman.

I never knew what she saw in my uncle or even how they first met. For his part, he hardly ever spoke about her. But they were together, after a fashion, for almost ten years. She was a large but handsome woman who towered over Uncle Dave—a kind of Joan Blondell type. Because of all the manuscripts that kept crossing her desk, and because of the company she kept during daylight hours, she became somewhat theatrical herself, always using words like "outstanding," and "superior." If she saw something she liked it was "simply outstanding," and if she saw something she thought you should like, it became "superior" to everything else. But, on the other hand, Frank, she knew every bookie by name and could find the powder room at the Copa during a blackout. She and Uncle Dave were a perfect fit, if you ask me. Although, I know for a fact, that my Uncle cheated on her shamelessly, usually with one or another of the "beautiful kids" who Dave seemed certain was going to be the next Carole Lombard.

Then one evening, very late at night, Carla's phone starts ringing.

She doesn't answer it at first, thinking it's a wrong number and that the caller will soon hang up. After about ten rings, she gets out of bed to answer the phone. "Hello. Who is this?" Carla asks. There is only silence on the other end of the phone, then the crying of a baby comes over the line.

"Who is this? What do you want?" Carla is about to hang up when a woman's voice says, "Carla Page, I want you to hear the sound of Dave Finkelstein's baby. Dave Finkelstein's baby is crying. I just thought you should know."

Carla never spoke to Uncle Dave after that phone call, Frank. I saw her at the funeral, but she never spoke to him again. When I asked Uncle Dave about this, he said, "Boychick," (that's what he always called me, even after Nancy Ava was born), "boychick, in the life of a man there are some things that should remain unsaid."

I had obviously crossed a line with him at that moment, Frank. He looked at me like Nathan admonishing David, and turned the cigar over in his mouth.

At the funeral, I even looked around for a young woman with a baby in her arms. But all I saw were some of the same guys I saw staring at their matchbooks when Dave sat down to join them at the Leisure Club and started up a conversation— about the new Pennsylvania Station, or Sherman Adams and his Vicuna coat—a conversation that only Uncle Dave was prepared to finish.

Your pal,

Fink

Dear Frank,

Earl Wilson was one of the so-called mourners at Uncle Dave's funeral a few months back. Dave's pallbearers looked like the kind of crowd who would've turned his coffin into a poker table if there'd been a pack of cards lying around from "Las Vegas Night" at temple Beth El. Earl Wilson came up to me after we left the service, Frank, and when I asked him how you were doing, he said he wouldn't know because the two of you are no longer speaking.

He said you would refuse to do a show if you knew Wilson was out front. He claims that you had him barred because he'd written something you didn't like. When I asked him what it was, he told me that it had something to do with the Weisman incident.

"Well, no wonder there's no cordiality left in your dealings with Frank," I told him. "The damage to Frank's reputation has already been done."

When I first heard about what happened that night, I kicked myself for having checked out of the Beverly Hills Hotel after getting into an argument with the manicurist at the hotel barber shop. Frank, I could tell she was getting great satisfaction turning down certain customers, and making it almost impossible to make an appointment for a manicure. When she asked to see my nails, as if I had to pass inspection first before she would consider working on me, I just saw red. First she tells me how crowded her schedule book is, then she suggests a barber shop in another hotel downtown. "This is all very helpful," I tell her, "but I happen to be staying at this particular hotel, and that I have an important customer to meet later in the day and I don't want to look like I've just come out of the coal mines of West

Virginia." I was good and sore, Frank, and wondered what kind of judge you had to be to qualify for a haircut in this joint.

To add insult to injury, Francis, she bursts out laughing when I show her my hands. I'm triple-jointed, Frank, and during a humid day, which this happened to have been, my hands were bent up like two snow plows.

"Those are two of the strangest-looking hands I've ever seen," she tells me. "I'm not sure I would even know what to do with them."

"I'm triple jointed, and in the army I did some boxing. Are you this helpful to all your customers?" I ask her.

"What are you inferring?" she asks.

"What I'm inferring, you who makes with the big words, is that this joint is more exclusive than a Mississippi lunch counter." I thought I was going to blow my stack in the place, Frank. I saw red, that's all I can say. But who do you think was getting a facial and a manicure at the same time, Frank, while I was having puppies over by the main reception area? The Duke.

Not Ellington, Frank, but the guy who gave up being the King of England "for the woman he loved." I noticed his wife sitting in the lobby on my way out of the hotel, Frank. She was sitting waiting for the Duke, holding two Pekinese, one under each arm. She doesn't look like she's changed much after all these years, still has a figure like an ironing board, if you ask me, but no one does.

So after that catastrophe in the hotel spa, Frank, I decided to leave the Beverly Hills and move to the Wilshire. So I missed all the excitement of that night when you and Dean, Richard Conte, Jilly and a few ladies who shall remain amphibious, walked into the Polo Lounge for some elbow bending in honor of Dean's forty-ninth.

The lounge was where we had Nancy Ava's sweet sixteen Party, Frank. But I realize now that it was a selfish thing for me to have it there. With all of Nancy Ava's friends back in New York, she wound up with a sweet sixteen party attended mostly by strangers—a regional sales manager up from San Francisco, Jill of course, and Milo, the Polo Lounge's maitre d'. It wasn't much fun for her, I'm afraid, Frank. The high point of the party for her was getting to kiss Burt Lancaster on the cheek. He was having lunch at a nearby table.

But I digress, Francis. I'm sorry I wasn't there that night for another reason. I think I could've prevented the fight with Weisman from the very beginning. You see, Frank, Frederick R. Weisman is a personal friend of Rosalie's husband Geoffrey Haines—the two men used to play golf together at least once a month along with Weisman's brother-in-law, Norton Simon. I met Frederick Weisman on one occasion as Rosalie's escort when they reopened, Peacock Alley in the Waldorf and brought Cole Porter's personal piano down from his penthouse after he passed away. I was surprised to see the president of Hunt's Food drinking at the bar. He seemed like an affable enough guy at the time, an interested listener with a laugh that was more like a grunt, as if somebody had told him a joke on the squash court.

When I read that it was Frederick R. Weisman who had

gotten into an altercation with you and the boys, I have to tell you, Frank, I cringed. The circumstances still seem hazy to me, Francis, but if I understand correctly, Weisman, who was sitting nearby with another guy whose name I've forgotten, leaned over and asked you to keep it down, and to watch your language because it might offend some of the women in the room. They say you told him he was out of line, and then, Frank, they say you made some comment about the guy being a Jew.

I can't believe that, Frank. Though when Weisman came over to your table to object, that's when the papers say you or someone at your table threw a telephone at the guy's head.

When you went into hiding for those two weeks while Weisman was in a coma—I don't know about you, Frank, but until Fred Weisman came to, and started recognizing members of his family again, I couldn't leave the house. I was never that scared before, Frank. For you, for Fred Weisman, for all of us. It's bad enough, Frank, to see the streets fill up with young people who never knew that for the last twenty years you were the best companion a guy could have. Not only do they not know how much you meant to our love life, today they would not believe it. But then it might be hard to believe, with only the news of the last few weeks to go on.

It came as a real relief, Frank, your statement to the Beverly Hills Police that the fight was all Weisman's fault. That he was the one who used profanity, and was the first to take a swing at you. It was like manna from heaven to hear you say you never hit the guy and that he knocked himself out by falling across the table. The stuff about calling Weisman "a Jew" doesn't seem like you, Frank. Not after all you've done for Jewish causes. Like Sammy Davis, going to Israel to be in *Cast a Giant Shadow*, and dating Angie Dickinson (or didn't you know, Frank)?

In fact, between you, me, and the lamppost, Francis, Fred Weisman is what happened when the Hunt brothers of Texas were accused of being anti-Semitic. They quickly hired Fred Weisman to run their company, even though (Rosalie told me) Weisman tried not once but on two separate occasions to get into the New York Athletic Club by sitting with the board of directors in their smoking room with a bottle of scotch, trying to convince them that he wasn't really Jewish. Rosalie heard from her husband Geoffrey Haines that Weisman had actually tried to make a case for himself by telling the board of directors that one of Hitler's closest "associates" was a guy named Rosenberg. I'm sure any hesitancy the admissions committee might've had completely vanished at the mention of Hitler as a character reference for Frederick R. Weisman. What was the guy thinking, Frank?

I can't tell you how relieved I am that Fred Weisman will live to see his daughter married by Buddy Hackett's rabbi and that I can leave the house and show my face around Hillview. (That's the country club we started when they wouldn't let us into Pineview—now everyone wants to get into Hillview, Frank. Even Jack Paar!)

But I have to tell you, Francis, those two weeks when Fred Weisman was in Mt. Sinai were hell. Nancy Ava and some of

Jill's old friends came over to keep the vigil with me. We just stayed in the house and played backgammon all day. We didn't go anywhere. We were like prisoners, Frank, waiting for Weisman to get up from his hospital bed. It was like a death watch. I have to say it was the first time I felt like I was cast out from Sinatraland, Frank, and the awful thing was, I didn't know why.

I'm sorry, Francis, but I had to let you know how I feel. According to the law of averages, we'll still come out ahead.

Your pal,

Finkie

Dear Frank,

After the Fred Weisman incident, I decided I had to get away. My brother was going to Miami and invited me to go down with him. Myron is a genius, Frank, at getting his friends to sponsor him for all sorts of freebies. This time it was as a guest of his friend Blinkie, who was involved in some sort of time share scam right off of Collins Avenue.

Myron can be a pill on vacation, but before I knew what hit me we were driving to LaGuardia, in separate cars, I might add, giving me the chance like a condemned man to think my own thoughts, something that with Myron around, I wouldn't be able to do for the next two weeks. Of course, even then, the decision to travel to the airport in two separate cars became the basis for a protracted argument, with Myron quoting actuarial tables as to the number of travelers involved in traffic accidents, due to jetlag driving home from the airport. I thanked him for his concern and got into my own car.

Even with his big belly and groaning about his spastic colon, Myron is, to this day, Frank, a remarkable athlete. Myron's one of these people who complain about the precariousness of their health—at the funerals of their friends.

We've been here for less than twenty-four hours and he's already beaten me twice at squash. In fact, Francis, I'm writing this from Blinkie's club, where Myron and I have just taken two of the longest and hottest showers on record. I'm sitting at the locker room table nursing a gin and ginger ale. I could lie down on this floor and go right to sleep, Frank, but I wanted to write to you instead. I've been feeling a little funny since the Weisman thing, and didn't want you to feel that the time has come, or anything, for a parting of the ways. I'm the only one here right now, so I can safely say that if a guy can feel real love for another guy without having to have his head examined, then I love you, Frank.

It's strange here now. It's a little like closing time at the Copa—I can hear sounds coming from the kitchen where the staff is having an early supper. There's even that frying pan smoke in the air, where the old guys who've worked here forever are cooking their dinner, just a few feet, but a whole lifetime, a whole generation of prosperity, away. I'm surrounded by these green steel lockers, Frank, like the ones we used to lean against at A.J. Demerast High, (though I know you only lasted

uable, whatever the duty on it was going to be, we cer-
ould have afforded it.

as really furious with Jill for risking so much on a silly
m sure she would've just thrown it into her jewelry box at
anyway, and never even worn it again. It was a strange
or a rich girl like Jill to have done. I wanted to tell her how
was but I didn't want the other people on the plane to
what was going on, so I kept my mouth shut. But I tell
rank, it wasn't easy.

he funny thing is, I remember going off to buy the ring for
e day of our anniversary. The girl who sold it to me looked
like Carolyn Jones, your co-star in A Hole in the Head.
old me, if I remember correctly, that it was an opal. She
that if you wear an opal ring it acts like coffee, in that it
rs you up. Well, I'm writing to tell you, Frank, it doesn't.
atever magical powers it's supposed to have, it just gave Jill
of her crazier ideas, and it sure wasn't much help in keeping
ogether.

If you ask me, Frank, Jill got spoiled going through customs
srael, our first stop. First, because a cousin of mine, Avraham
ffe, whisked us through at the airport. He was a newly mint-
hero of the Suez Canal, Frank, in '56 (I think he knew Mickey
rcus, and Ben Dunkelman, the guy you played when you
nt over there to be in Cast a Giant Shadow).

Avraham Yoffe was in the Israeli cabinet when Jill and I
sited. So we got V.I.P. treatment as soon as we stepped off the
ane. We stayed at the King David Hotel and sipped our

for forty-two days). A miserable little lamp is hanging from the
ceiling. Why do locker rooms always make me doubt my life?

I'm sure you've felt this way, Frank, coming in after a day at
the Bing Crosby Classic. I can't think of how many men a mil-
lion times over have felt this way, sitting in their boxer shorts, a
little groggy from too much Bombay gin and Canada Dry. But
I'm not drunk, just at that point where I can speak bluntly to a
friend. You can trust me, Frank, you can write to me in complete confidence. I know you've been a little reluctant to do it
after so many years of not responding to my letters. It would be
a shame to break the streak just to get something off your chest,
but I want you to know that you can do it: blow the ash off your
cigarette and start a letter to Finkie. I mean a guy like you,
Frank, you have too many damn friends in this town. If you con-
fided in any one of them they'd call a press conference, which
I'm sure is the last thing you'd want.

Myron actually put me up to telling you that, Francis. He's
always trying to get me to screw up my courage to say something
that needed to be said, or to do something that no one else
wants to do—but usually, Frank, instead of screwing up my
courage he just screws me up.

Like with Rosalie, for example. Myron is trying to get me to
visit Rosalie, who happens to be back here now, reunited with
her husband, Geoffrey Haines. They live in Boca Raton in a
house with a driving range that Rosalie's husband designed for
himself. I don't know if Myron has a clear conscience about trying to get me to visit Rosalie. Sometimes I think he encourages

me to do the wrong thing, just so he could tell me that he was right all along and that he, Myron, my brother, is the only true friend I've ever had and will ever need. I hope I'm wrong about that one, Frank. I'd hate to think Myron is taking advantage of a bad situation like that.

But it does seem strange, doesn't it, Frank, that on the way over to the club, Myron starts to engage me in what went wrong with my relationship, not just with Rosalie but with Jill, someone I know he never cared for that much to begin with. When Myron asked me, "Where do you think things went wrong with you and Jill?" I'll admit I took the bait and told him what I thought in one word—"pregnant."

That's not to say that I don't love Nancy Ava. Frank, like you, I think the world of my "Nancy with the Laughing Face." In fact you would've been proud of our Nancy sitting in front of the television rooting for your Nancy to win the Grammy award for "Boots"—Nancy Ava is crazy for that tune, Francis. I mean we're as patriotic as the next guy, Frank, but when Barry Sadler beat out Nancy Jr. for the Grammy with that song about the Green Berets, Nancy Ava groaned with disappointment and turned the set off in disgust. In fact, Frank, Nancy Ava told us that most of the soldiers in Vietnam prefer "These Boots Are Made for Walking" to "Ballad of the Green Berets." She said they like to play it over loudspeakers on all the army bases and from the decks of the aircraft carriers as the planes take off on their bombing missions. You must be very proud of Nancy Jr., Frank.

But there was a wall, Frank, th[...]
us when Jill became pregnant. May[...]
way of looking at me, as if I was the[...]
denly.

Myron certainly was no help eith[...]
ous arguments tended to be about hi[...]
for insinuating himself into the relati[...]
most vulnerable. Around the time of[...]
before we bought our house, that type[...]
under the guise of his trying to help us,[...]
cal advice. All of this from a guy with p[...]
buys plastic shoes and until recently live[...]
apartment we lived in when we were kid[...]
started about Myron, Frank. As Jill once s[...]
al quicksand—first I fall in and then wh[...]
pull me out, they get sucked in too.

Except for Myron, Jill and I never reall[...]
per se. I remember once, we were coming[...]
Israel and Turkey and Jill tried to smuggle in[...]
her as an anniversary present. I was filling[...]
give you on the plane when I just forgot ab[...]
about to ask for another customs form fr[...]
when Jill squeezed my arm like it was a cuff i[...]
machine. She told me that she wasn't going t[...]
She even had it turned around so that it look[...]
band or something. I thought it was a pretty[...]
What was so baffling to me, Frank, was that th[...]

that va[...]
tainly [...]
I [...]
ring. I'[...]
home,[...]
thing[...]
mad [...]
know[...]
you, [...]
Jill th[...]
a lot[...]
She [...]
said[...]
sobe[...]
Wh[...]
one[...]
us t[...]
in [...]
Yo[...]
ed[...]
M[...]
we[...]
vi[...]
p[...]

Campari and soda on the deck overlooking the Old City, which is still in Jordanian hands, in other words, off limits. Avraham told us that if there's ever another war, Frank, Israel will take the Old City back.

Why did Jill care, after that, about saving a hundred bucks? I'll never figure it out. It wasn't even her money. She was always unpredictable. She could turn on a dime. I used to think that maybe she had a metal plate in her head that she never told me about. I read once where having a metal plate in your head could affect your personality, making you touchy and unpredictable. Maybe I was the one with the plate in my head, Frank.

I remember the day I had to take Jill to the hospital, the day Nancy Ava was born. It was very cold that day, Frank. I think I heard later that it was the coldest day in New York, ever. I put every coat and sweater we owned around her and then walked her out to the car. She made some wisecrack about how the hospital was just uptown, not in Alaska. It was the kind of remark she made whenever she was upset about something. The way some people start singing when they're nervous. Jill made sarcastic little jokes. When we arrived at the hospital, the nurse and I tried to help Jill out of the pile of coats, jackets, and cardigans I had thrown on her. I tried to make myself useful but the more I did, the more annoyed she seemed to become. I asked her if there was anything she's like to read while she waited for the doctor to arrive, and she said, "Yeah, how about an illustrated history of the Finkelstein family?" I was starting to feel like an idiot for sticking around.

The nurse took all the coats and sweaters away. When she finally came back into the room Jill was furiously smoking a cigarette. She looked like a pregnant version of Bette Davis in *All About Eve*. The nurse asked Jill to please put out her cigarette. Jill, who always had a lot of power, threw her cigarette case at the nurse and connected. It hit the nurse right on her bosom. The nurse then told me that she thought it would be best if I left the room. Now, I'd seen Olivia de Havilland in *Snake Pit*, Frank, and I was worried. I imagined the two women going at it right there in the maternity ward, with the baby being born in the middle of a cat fight. At one point the nurse came out to tell me that if Jill didn't calm down they might have to restrain her.

I was there when they brought Nancy Ava to Jill's room. I'll never forget it, Frank, as long as I live or don't live. Jill looked at the baby, and then looked up at me with the most sour expression on her face, like she had been sucking on a lemon instead of looking down at her baby for the first time. For the next year I never saw Jill look at Nancy Ava the way you would imagine a mother would look at her child. I can't remember her ever picking Nancy Ava up out of her crib, preferring Mrs. Ashe, the maid the Bronsteins loaned us to help Jill out for those first few months, to hold the baby until she fell asleep. Of course, she refused to breast feed. I didn't have any problem with that, Frank. A lot of women are funny about that. It's just that for the life of me I couldn't figure out what any of us had done to deserve this. I even asked Nancy's doctor, Bob Harding, a decent guy who never gets rattled by anything, his opinion of what was going on. He said that as far as Jill is concerned, I was really in for it. He said that it was an unpredictable thing and that every woman was different. He told me that some women bounce back from this sort of problem more quickly than others after they have a baby. He said, and I quote, that "It can take a while before the machinery is back in its proper place." Well, whatever was going on with Jill, Frank, whatever was wrong, it was becoming pretty obvious that her "machinery" had nothing to do with it. I'm sure it all started before a couple of washers got loose.

I'm afraid it was me, Frank. It was me. My timing was way off. When Jill would be in the mood to get all dressed up and have me take her out to dinner, I would be mentally looking forward to loosening my belt and watching Archie Moore fight on television. When I thought that I finally talked her into taking up golf and learning how to drive, she was taking up drinking and reading books thick as New York steaks, like *The Robe* or *The Carpetbaggers*.

But more importantly, I could tell she didn't like being in Sinatraland anymore. When I first met Jill, I liked the fact that she had a wild and willful streak, that she threw her shoes off to dance with me, that she knew all the words to *Songs for Swingin' Lovers*. Even after Nancy Ava came along I loved the fact that she always "outdressed," if that's the word, all the other young mothers we knew. I can't say that we ever made any real close friends in those days, Frank. As a young couple we spent a lot of time at her father's club. I hope you don't mind my telling you,

Frank, that there were a lot of heated conversations about your friendships with Willie Moretti and Frank Costello. I even had to defend your hanging around with Sammy Cahn, when Mrs. Epsteen (that's her spelling not mine) said that Sammy refused her invitation to sit at their table at the Chez Paree to toast their daughter's twenty-first birthday. Apparently, Sammy said, sitting with the Epsteens was something he could "live without."

Opinions like that put us on the outs with a lot of people Jill had known before our marriage. In the beginning she would never have allowed that kind of thing to get to her, but after a while, she began to change, Frank. Even her look began to change. She started dressing more conservatively, in suits and dresses that looked like they were designed by Omar the tent maker. As Joe E. Lewis once said, Frank, she "joined the throng." It was strictly the early show. No encores.

For the longest time, I kept all this from Myron. At first, I thought he would get too much satisfaction out of watching my marriage to Jill come apart at the seams. This development would have only served to bolster Myron's contention that he was the only person in my life I could ever rely on. That sooner or later everyone I came in contact with was bound to disappoint me. Jill, Nancy Ava, Rosalie. All of them. I started to think a terrible thought, that the end of my marriage secretly delighted my brother because it left us the way we were after our parents were gone, when we shared that tiny apartment at the foot of the George Washington Bridge.

I never asked Myron for anything, even when I needed money after Jill's father refused to give us that birthday present he had been threatening to bestow on us. I refused to come to Myron for a hand out. I never doubted that he would give me the money if I asked for it. I would never question his loyalty, Frank. I know how much loyalty means to you. That's the only way to explain Corbett Monica, Frank. Because I have to say, I saw him on the Sullivan show last week, and I know that he's been opening for you all over the country for the last couple of years, but Frank, he's not funny! When I mentioned this to Allen Munshin, the maitre d' at Patsy's, he told me the story about how Corbett Monica's mother was the last person to see you before your gall bladder surgery, and how you vowed that if you came through it all right, her son would be your opening act for as long as you performed. So I know something about loyalty, Frank. And Myron is nothing if not loyal. But I didn't want to give him the chance to lord it over me. To tell me that I couldn't go to Vegas because I had to borrow some money from him and that "borrowers can't afford to be gamblers," and all that kind of horseshit. Also, I didn't want to feel obligated to him in any way. After my divorce, Myron did offer to give me a considerable amount of money when I was thinking of incorporating myself—but I never asked. I know that you're known for your generosity, Frank, but doesn't it ever feel like a burden to have so many people around who want to pay you back but can't? People like Jilly Rizzo, for example.

I know for a fact that Jilly can't go anywhere, he feels so obligated to you. Even if he wanted to pay you back for all your kindness he couldn't afford to. So in a way, Francis, like Myron, you get more out of being generous than we do. You get a life-time of loyalty and favors. We get infusions of cash when we need it. If you want to get ahead in the world, taking money like that is a bad deal because it creates loyalty and loyalty only winds up nailing your feet to the floor.

I was commuting from New Rochelle to the office, with Jill and Nancy Ava spending the afternoons together. I was looking after a successful business, but in reality Myron had me back in short pants learning my Haftorah. You see, the money I did wind up taking from Myron, Frank, was the umbilical cord he used to draw me closer to him. As you discovered with Dolly, umbilical cords can reach around the world. It can strangle you while you're on tour, sitting in a penthouse in Perth, Australia just as easily as it can strangle you in the womb. That's probably why I find myself here, taking this vacation with Myron, and why, even though I spent most of this letter talking about my marriage, I find myself thinking about Rosalie. My last way out.

She's someone beyond the grasp of Myron's jealous nature. All the mistakes in that relationship are mine, Frank. And that's why I'm thinking of going to see her tomorrow. Maybe her instincts will tell her something different. Maybe I don't have a chance. But I'm prepared to ask Rosalie to marry me, I'll tell her what you told Harry Cohn when you wanted the part of Maggio in *From Here to Eternity*, "I'll pay you to let me play that role."

Your pal,

Finkie

Dear Frank,

I never did see Rosalie again. We'll never have that reunion I'd been fantasizing about since Myron and I came down here. I told myself that I absolutely had to succeed with her. That there was no turning back. Maybe a lot of it was my own vanity, the way we had broken up, with her sister in the room like some Spanish duenna. Maybe it was all about the past and how hard it is to let go. Maybe it was her voice, the voice of a shy girl whom the troubles of the world had poured into. Did I ever tell you, Frank, about the time Rosalie took me to her husband's cabana in Mystic and how she kissed me and then vanished and how I went to look for her and all these other people all dressed up for dinner started to look at me as I ran through the place in my shorts like a crazy person looking in every room in the world? I was afraid she would forget me, with the sun quickly burning itself out in the sky. It was the scariest day of my life.

Every day since we got here I've thought about what it would be like to walk down Fourteenth Street in the winter with Rosalie leaning against me for warmth, kissing her hair, the moon coming into its own in the sky. We would pass a record store and the radio would be on and you would be singing to us "That's Life." "I pick myself up and get back in the race. That's life. That's what people say."

I adored Rosalie, Frank. But I didn't know that fate wanted me to make the rest of the trip alone. I'm just a man who thought he was crazy about a girl. But I was just crazy.

I was so excited when Rosalie agreed to see me. I couldn't

think of anything but her. Even Myron with his dark skin and brown eyes made me think of her. It never occurred to me that Rosalie might have wanted to be with Geoffrey Haines, or that she had agreed to see me just to say that she was still in love with her husband and out of courtesy wanted to tell me that in person. It never entered my mind—as you would say, Frank— that perhaps Haines would have something to say about all of this. That he would find my fantasies about going off with his wife not very romantic after all. I don't know whether or not it ever occurred to me that Rosalie was even married—I mean, really married—to Geoffrey Haines.

With Nancy Ava in college and my life with Jill more of a mirage than ever, Rosalie seemed to exist for me like an actress on the big screen. Every gesture and look of her I could recall seemed larger than life, which is kind of like saying she doesn't really exist for me at all. Suddenly, it seemed that we had been apart for a very long time.

Rosalie and I liked to travel together. I remember what a thrill it was to drive out of the city. The New York skyline not letting us see anything else, then suddenly vanishing. And we found ourselves on the Henry Hudson Parkway listening to Milton Gross on the radio as the curtain came up on the Metropolitan Opera and Robert Merrill's voice made the world a little less dark. Rosalie would grab my arm as if no one else's touch could warm her. I felt like a great man then, Frank. I was playing with life the way you play with an audience, or the way you tease a song out of its hiding place. The big difference is, you know what you're doing, Frank. For me, its strictly pretend.

It's almost morning, Frank, and so I know that it's real, that what happened isn't something I dreamed up sitting at the bottom of a glass of gin. I thought I would watch myself, that I would be careful and be able to forget all about it. But you can't forget it when the world turns cold and you don't know what is coming to take its place. But whatever it is, I hope I can breathe in it.

As I told the detectives who came to the bungalow to question me, I don't have any more information about what happened than anyone else who happened to pick up a newspaper over the last few days. No one will ever know exactly what happened the afternoon Haines returned from that business trip. The driver of a school bus for handicapped kids saw Haines standing in a kind of daze in the middle of his circular driveway. That was around four o'clock in the afternoon. At five Haines called the Miami police and told them to come to the house and pick him up. When they arrived they found Rosalie stretched out on the sofa in the sun room like someone who had fallen asleep while reading a book.

The day before, when I spoke to Rosalie, she told me that Geoffrey was in Pensacola on business but that he would be back late the next day. She agreed to see me and we arranged to meet at Victor's at three o'clock. Victor's is a Cuban joint mostly deserted at that hour, Frank, so we thought it would ensure our privacy.

I couldn't tell over the phone what Rosalie expected from

our meeting. Did she want one final get-together to tell me the truth about what she thought of me, or our relationship? Or was she simply using me to complain about her husband, who was spending more and more time away from the house? Was it simply loneliness, or—worse—boredom?

You could understand, Frank, why I had to see her. It was the only way to answer these questions for myself, to say nothing of having the thing you long for and fear.

When Rosalie failed to show up at Victor's I drove to the Haines' house, right on the edge of that driving range he had built for himself.

I had pictured the house Rosalie had been sharing with Geoffrey Haines, in much the same way I had imagined Rosalie living in the house with him, moving past the blank walls, reaching for a cigarette from the low table in front of the sofa. I knew the place itself from Rosalie's description of how she spent most of her time reading in a small nook at the side of the house. I know it sounds strange, Frank, but I feel I was guided there by the thought of her sitting and reading a book.

What I found, Frank, were about sixteen cop cars and a black van from the Miami Coroner's office.

The only thing I remember hearing was my own heart pumping blood into my ears, so that it sounded like I was back at the ocean with all the windows open.

I got out of the car, Frank, although I knew I shouldn't have. I didn't go near the house. I just stumbled along the sidewalk and leaned against a palm tree. I don't think I started crying. But I did do something pretty strange, Frank. I took two of the dead palms that had fallen from the tree and started to rub them against the tree, to put them back where they belonged. I kept doing this until my hands started to burn and then they started to bleed, but I still tried to put the giant leaves back on the tree.

As I walked back to the car, I thought I heard Haines screaming, I thought I heard him cry out. Maybe I just imagined it. I drove home very slowly, Frank. All of a sudden, I became afraid that something was going to happen to me. At this point I had no idea that Rosalie was in any danger. But I made no attempt to try and call her, either.

I don't think I'm going to be charged with any type of crime, but a fellow here from the District Attorney's office tells me that I'm going to probably have to testify at some kind of hearing into what happened. A coroner's inquest, I think they call it.

I can hear Myron's voice in the next room, Frank. I'm barely able to stand on my own two feet, but I think I should go to him. He's probably more scared than the two of us put together. And don't you worry about me, pal. Just think about someone who liked to sit on her bed surrounded by flowered hats, just think of Rosalie, the next time you do "The Most Beautiful Girl in the World."

Your pal,

Fink

Dear Frank,

Every man over fifty should watch his weight, Frank, but I don't recommend losing weight the way I did. I call it "The Dead Man's Diet." I hope you never go on it. I didn't go on it on purpose, it happened gradually. After Rosalie's death I just lost interest in food. Even my divorce didn't bother me the way that Rosalie's murder haunted my sleep.

I was compelled to testify as a material witness, Frank. But that had more to do with the fact that I was probably one of the last people to speak with Rosalie.

The jury found Haines not guilty of Rosalie's murder, but back in New York, Frank, you would've thought that I was the one charged with her murder, not Haines. There were so many lawyers objecting to one thing or another during my two days on the witness stand that the transcript of the trial has only one or two pages of my testimony on it.

I don't know why people think the things they do, Frank. I feel as though I've been convicted of something terrible by the people I live with, by my neighbors, by the people I run into at work or on the street. Because Haines was such a prominent man, the newspapers in Miami and New York had a field day with the story. One paper, I think it was the *Daily News*, even referred to me as "the aging swinger who was the murdered woman's lover." It was quite an ordeal, Frank. Now I know what you must've gone through when you refused to testify before the New Jersey State Commission in their investigations into organized crime. And then *The Godfather* came out! We were both on trial, Frank.

We all knew Haines had killed Rosalie, Frank. We all knew about his terrible temper and his jealousy. Geoffrey Haines was one of the men, Frank, who meets his wife in a nightclub, admiring her tits one day and then, six months after the wedding, when they're getting ready to go out, he sees his wife wearing the same low cut dress she was wearing the night they met, only this time with a strand of pearls that he gave her as a wedding present,. And he says to her, "You're not going out in that are you?" accusing her of dressing just for the men at the party. Haines was that kind of clod, Frank.

Of course, I will always feel partly to blame for what happened. Perhaps if it wasn't for me, Haines wouldn't have had any reason to suspect his wife of being unfaithful. There may be some truth in what I say, or it may be that the truth is out of reach. But like you, I had already convicted and sentenced myself before I ever took the stand. I just waited for the people I knew and loved to come to their senses. I even offered to release my customers from their obligations to me until they felt comfortable enough to do business again. I thought they would come around eventually, Frank. But as of today I'm still waiting for them to return to the fold.

A couple of younger kids just coming up took advantage of my temporary disgrace to steal some of my business away from me. It's pretty disillusioning, Frank, to see people you thought were your friends act with such cowardice.

But the only person who could claim to have really suffered

here, Frank, is Rosalie. Geoffrey Haines can go back to being the "Frank Lloyd Wright of golf," but Rosalie can't go back, Frank. She won't even have the satisfaction of thinking what a botch she'd made of her life. At least when you're sobbing, Frank, you usually know what the reason is, and the reason is usually because you're alive and cannot avoid the pain of it. Isn't that right, Francis?

Things were getting so bad, Frank, that I thought I'd have to sell my golf clubs and move into a furnished room above a bus station like in *The Man with the Golden Arm*. I was starting to think that I was some sort of a reverse Midas, Frank. Everything I touched turned into shit.

But I know that that's not going to be the case forever. I keep telling myself that people do have the time to be compassionate. Today, for the first time in a long while, Frank, I felt as if I was coming back to life again. It was in the Port Authority bus terminal, a young woman I'd never seen before was behind the counter selling tickets. I could tell that she was getting ready to finish her shift and another woman was standing next to her, about to take her place. I said a silent prayer that she would still be there when it was my turn to buy the bus ticket. I don't think I ever wanted anything as badly as I wanted to stand in front of this woman and receive a sign that justice is tempered with mercy.

In a way, Rosalie's death, or should I say the scandal that came after it, turned out to be a kind of release in the sense that I no longer worry what people think about me. I am unembarrasable, Frank. That's why I can tell you that it doesn't bother me that it's been something of a one-way street all these years, all these unanswered letters. But I still say the same prayer every night: "Thank God for Frank Sinatra. Thank God for Jilly Rizzo. How did all these people get in my room?"

Your pal,

Finkie

Dear Frank,

Just before we left Miami, Myron and I ran into Ben Novak and his shadow at the Fountainbleau. I can never remember the guy's name, but Ben is always whispering to him in the lobby or by the side of the pool. Ben seemed to know, even before the newspapers, about Rosalie's murder.

Ben asked if there was anything he could do for me.

"Sure," I said, "can you get me a new girlfriend?" I immediately thought to myself, Finkie, what a stupid thing to have said to a guy who's only trying to help you. But when you consider the strain I was under during that time, Frank, I'm sure you'd understand. The amazing thing, Francis, was that Ben didn't know I was kidding. He took out a business card and wrote something down on the back of it, then he handed it to me. "Tell her Uncle Ben sent you," he said. I think Ben really wanted to set me up with some girl he knew who worked for him at the hotel.

A few weeks after we arrived back in New York, I read that

Ben Novak and his shadow were being cited by the U.S. Attorney in Washington as being fronts for substantial investments of mob money. Ben Novak, Frank! I remember Ben Novak when he was entertainment director at Kutsher's up in the Catskill Mountains! It's hard to imagine him doing his own laundry, never mind the mob's.

Nancy Ava came home from college, Frank, because the whole school was shut down on account of protests against the war. Nancy said that she read somewhere that you were the only one in Hollywood to come out for Humphrey. She said Shirley MacLaine and Sammy Davis Jr. were campaigning for Bobby Kennedy and that Robert Vaughn and Dick Van Dyke were supporting Eugene McCarthy. Nancy Ava told me she saw a debate in which Gregory Peck debated Charlton Heston on the war in Vietnam. She said Gregory Peck was still handsome and made some very good points about why it took Kennedy so long to come out against the war. I told Nancy that you would never support Bobby Kennedy because of the way he helped to turn his brother away from you and because he sent Mr. Giancana to prison. In fact, I remember Ben Novak telling me in the lobby of the Fountainbleu Hotel that you told him that if Bobby Kennedy were elected president, "We'd all be under arrest."

Nancy Ava is what they call an "activist," Frank. She wants us to get the hell out of Vietnam. She's already been arrested twice for blocking the entrance to the induction center. Last night we were about to go out to dinner when I mentioned to her that I thought she might want to take off those dark socks because they didn't look right with the cream colored dress she was wearing. She told me that those weren't socks I was looking at, that was hair. Nancy Ava said that she and some of her friends at school were refusing to shave their legs until the end of the war. I asked her if she knew how her mother felt about this, because I remembered how fastidious Jill used to be about shaving her legs. It made me think of the white razor with the thin gold stripe running down the side that I always saw in the soapdish beside the bath. She said that Jill didn't mention anything about the hair on her legs, but said that she hoped Nancy Ava would go on the pill if she intended to sleep with anyone at school. That's quite a piece of advice to give your little girl, don't you think, Frank? Well, at least she wasn't trying to sell her dope.

Liquor and sex were enough for us, Francis. What else was there? I guess there were sleeping pills, but I was always afraid of them. It was too easy to overdose. Nancy Ava says that each year at school, at least two or three kids jump to their deaths off a bridge over the Connecticut River, either because of the strain of keeping up their grades or because of a bad love affair. I told Nancy Ava that our generation never wanted to die. We may have done some self-destructive things in our day, but we had a strong will to live, didn't we, Frank? Even people I knew who found themselves in the most degrading circumstances wanted to go on living.

I don't necessarily believe in Him. But I talk to God, sometimes, Frank. It beats the pants off talking to yourself.

Although you really are talking to yourself when you talk to God, aren't you, Francis? And when I find myself talking to Him, it's usually because I'm asking Him to keep me alive in one way or another. I hope you won't think I'm ready for the nuthouse, Frank, but when you pray to God that you can still do something well, something you've done a thousand times before, then you're praying to God to bring you back, like for an encore, you're praying for more life.

Speaking of encores, Frank, I read in the funny papers that you gave Nancy Jr. away, again, in marriage. In the photograph of you coming out of the church in Cathedral City, you looked just a little sad. Maybe it was the fact that your father wasn't there or maybe it was just the sun in your eyes, I couldn't be sure. I read that when you saw your son-in-law kneeling at the altar, you couldn't take your eyes off his shoes. That the soles were a pretty beige color and didn't have a scratch on them, like the shoes of a little boy dressed up to go out with his parents. Someone said you thought of sneaking up behind him with a crayon and writing "L" and "R" on them for left and right.

What is it about us, Frank, "we fathers of daughters"? I've always wondered why it's so hard, make that impossible, to strike the right balance between being the tough guy and the soft touch—George Raft and Judge Hardy. In the beginning, it's hard to be anything but a pushover. After all, Frank, how much of a hard case can you be with a three-year-old girl who shuffles into the bedroom in your size eleven wing tips? But then, before you know it she's six or seven, and she's swinging a twelve iron like a scythe in the living room and you're suddenly a cop asking a would-be bank robber to turn over his weapon. I can't think of anything I've ever done that was more demeaning than having to order Nancy Ava to do something. By the time she was maybe seven or eight years old, I was finished. She had won the day in the rules department. I hear other fathers say, "If only I had been tougher on her in the beginning, things would've been different." But I never felt that way, Frank. It was obvious to me from about the time she was ten years old that Nancy Ava was already determined to make men suffer. And that while none of us know what really goes on in the hearts of women, we do know that our daughters are judging us.

I sometimes wonder, Frank, if Nancy, your Nancy, was ever upset with you for being such an unconventional father. The fact that you never had to go to the same office every day, or even have the same telephone number from one week to the next? I had those things, Frank, but I don't think it made any difference. Nancy Ava never seemed to look to me for approval, Frank, just love. I'm sure you've had this same experience, with Nancy deciding to go into show business, of having a daughter who wanted to make her own decisions regardless of what you thought about it. I'd like to think that because I went to an office every day, and went from being a young man with a straight back to being a gray-haired man with a slight stoop, that somehow this made it easier for Nancy Ava to do certain things.

But I'm afraid this was wishful thinking on my part, Francis. Because according to all the experts, I was something less than a success as a father. Because it was so hard for me to tell Nancy that the world was full of suffering, I just left it out, like in the days when I used to read to her before bed and I'd come to a part in the story that I thought might give her nightmares, and so I would skip over it and go directly to the beautiful party in the castle with a charming prince somewhere in the picture. So in that way, I didn't do Nancy Ava any favors by shielding her from the dangers in life, but I did it, I know now, because I didn't want to face up to them myself.

Despite all the time we spent together, Frank, I think that Nancy Ava came to see me as a kind of phantom, someone she created as carefully and meticulously as she did her imaginary friend, Bacon. The father she thought she knew, the one who tapped his beard shavings into an empty cigar box, and the one who tucked her in at night, who had my brown eyes and my dark hair, that guy walking through the rooms of our house, sitting at Nancy's desk at school on parent's night, was a ghost haunting her life.

I know you once said that, "It was a father's duty to be a son-of-a-bitch." So that later on, our daughters will know what all men are capable of becoming. Well, its true, Frank, that not everything turns out alright in the morning. And that most guys who are shitheels at work are shitheels coming home from work. And that it doesn't matter what side of the bed he wakes up on, most men tell a whole lot of lies.

I was talking with someone once, Frank, on an airplane, who said that he walked around with the terrible feeling that his daughters hated him, and that there was nothing he could do about it except die, and that only the thought of his wife reacting to the news kept him from doing away with himself. I felt terrible for that man, Frank. But on the other hand, I can't say that I ever worried about whether or not my daughter felt I had somehow let her down, just because we were of two minds about something which seemed so important at the time. A ghost is incapable of disappointing, unless he simply fails to appear. And I always came home.

But I am fiercely proud of Nancy Ava, Frank. For in the years since our divorce, she has lived in two homes and done so with one heart. That itself is an act of incredible courage and will, though I think she is probably too young to appreciate it. And like any gift, your voice, for example, or playing the violin like Heifetz, it came out of her practically by accident, without her even recognizing it. That is the reason, Frank, why I speak of her with such admiration and with so much love.

Your pal,

Finkie

THE SECOND TIME AROUND

Dear Frank,

No one disappears unless they want to. So I guess I must've wanted some time to walk the streets of this old town by myself. That's probably why you didn't hear from me for a while. Also, it was a time for thinking about my life, Frank. Like you, Francis, I'm fifty-five and counting. I guess that and Jill's remarrying threw me off my game a little (She wound up with the son of one of her father's former business partners, an executive at Goodyear—I think they live in a suburb of Michigan, in a house they designed together in the shape of a huge tire).

I hear that you're planning on building a new house yourself, Frank, up in the mountains above Palm Springs. I wish I could get you to move to New York. I think you would like being a private person for a while. You can do that here, Frank.

Well, I'm going to stop nagging you about New York. I don't want you to move here under false pretenses—you'd still cause a sensation walking down 57th Street, and all the doormen along Fifth Avenue just above 60th Street will still call out your name, but here nobody really cares what you do, and most importantly, you won't have to care how you look to the public. (I once saw Kirk Douglas running out of the Plaza Hotel in his pajamas to pay someone's cabfare.) It'll give you a new kind of freedom from your own fame that you've never had before. But being fed up with the heat and all that smog isn't going to make you fall in love with New York, Frank. New York has it's problems, to be sure, but we're getting too old to demand perfection, Frank. But I've got to tell you, hugging the park on that long walk up Fifth around seven o'clock at night smack in the middle of autumn is really something. That's why I don't want to live anywhere else, Frank. Although Odette is trying to get us to move to Great Neck.

I just realized I never told you anything about Odette, have I, Francis? Well, it's one of the reasons I ceased being a juvenile, Frank—meeting Odette. It was nearly a year ago. I was passing in front of Le Pavillon when I saw two women having an argument. They were saying some pretty awful things about each other, Frank, and one of them started to drag a completely innocent third party who was just leaving the restaurant into this fight. That was Odette, Frank. I made like I was supposed to meet her there in front of the restaurant, and with those two battle axes looking on, I whisked Odette across the street. We've been together ever since.

It might amuse you to know, Frank, that Odette used to be a movie actress. People used to mistake her for Gloria Grahame, probably because of that protruding upper lip and her tendency to frown just before she speaks.

Odette made a lot of pictures, Frank, usually as the bad girl or as she likes to put it, "the town tramp." She started out in Judy Garland pictures like *Pigskin Parade.* You can see her in the football stands leading a cheer. Jimmy Stewart took her out a couple of times, Frank, and I think Henry Fonda, too. Odette says that Stewart is supposed to be worth about $30 million. I can't believe it, Frank. Thirty mill? Odette says that only Der Bingle is richer, and that's from oil, and orange juice and who the hell knows what else. No wonder he always looks so relaxed. He sure doesn't have to worry about blowing it all at Santa Anita. Odette says he's a silent partner there, too.

Odette had a pretty good run in Hollywood, Frank, until she was in her forties. In her last movie, before selling her house and moving to New York, she played an invalid who was being held prisoner by a bunch of juvenile delinquents. The star of the movie was Sal Mineo.

We live in a swanky apartment. Babe Ruth used to live here. His apartment is now occupied by Itzhak Perlman, the crippled violin player. The doorman always asks me if I'll be wanting a taxi. After a lifetime of hailing my own cabs, I feel a little funny having this guy step out into the street to blow his dog whistle, but I'm getting used to it.

Our place is smaller than some of the other apartments in the building, but it's full of nice things that Odette brought with her from Hollywood. I've even become interested in painting, thanks to Odette. Not just Al Hirschfeld's caricatures, but oil paintings. Odette has a Milton Avery hanging in the living room and a Raphael Soyer in the bedroom.

Most of Odette's money, the money she made from pictures, went into decorating her house on North Roxbury Drive in Beverly Hills. She was married to a set designer out there by the name of Dartagnan Cotton—Odette said she came home from the studio one day and found Dartagnan in bed with one of the young men he hired to drive him around. Apparently Odette's husband had once been a passenger in a car that drove off a bridge into a river and so he was never able to drive after that. But he certainly filled Odette's house with all kinds of beautiful things, Frank. Russian snuff boxes, mirrors of all shapes and sizes, a Tiffany clock that stopped running the year you left Harry James, and an oil painting of Odette in the role of a Confederate belle in a John Ford picture.

The one thing I brought with me from New Rochelle, Frank, was the portable bar, so you don't have to be afraid you'll die of thirst if you decide to visit us. It's a beauty, Francis, equipped with a matching ice bucket and cocktail shaker, monogrammed. A set of bottles that'll be around for awhile—made of the heaviest cut glass, each with its own solid gold label hanging around its neck on a chain. There's one for Scotch, one for bourbon, one for gin, vodka, vermouth and so on. Leave the St. Bernard at home, Frank, it's all here.

After the scandal surrounding Rosalie's murder, I lost a lot of my old customers, especially when my picture began appearing in the newspapers as "the mystery man in the killing of Rosalie Haines." Even if you're not guilty of something, Frank—and I know you can speak to this better than anyone—people want to judge you, and after they've judged you, there is nothing you can do to take away the ache of being misjudged. The chapel of the truly innocent is pretty small, Frank. I'm not sure who could get in there.

I thought about this a great deal after Rosalie's death. Especially when, as I said before, a lot of the younger reps took advantage of my self-imposed hiatus to steal my business. It got so bad that I was starting to accept more of these "gifts" from Myron, checks that would come in the mail for a couple of hundred dollars, and then a few thousand. But it was an intolerable situation, Frank, because no gift from my brother comes without strings. Like if I happen to mention to him that Odette and I were going off to a Broadway show, he would ask me in an almost casual way whether or not I thought that ticket prices for Broadway shows were too high, and wouldn't I be better off standing on line for cheaper tickets at that booth in the middle of Times Square? But what he was really getting at, Frank, was shouldn't I be more careful with my money, his money, and should someone whose business was hurting the way mine was be spending money on a Broadway show? This kind of thing went on all the time with him, Frank, and it got to the point where I had no choice but to get out of the drapery hardware business and do something desperate before I was living on handouts from my brother.

So I took what money I still had from the handful of customers I had left and invested it with a man I had known when I was married to Jill, a specialist in a few stocks who, on those rare occasions when I would visit him at his office, never seemed to be doing anything until the last half-hour before the market closed, when he somehow managed to make a profit. I never second guess the decisions he makes about the market, and so far, Frank, Odette and I haven't had the horrible experience of having to dip into our capital.

I even got into the habit of visiting the brokerage office every day but almost never going in. It's a ritual I do to insure the continued success of our investments. To silently wish him and us luck before the closing bell. As you might've guessed, it's one of those offices where you can see the brokers on the phone from the street, and where you can read the ticker tape on a screen, like the one along the top of the Time-Life Building in Times Square. Maybe that's why I always think about where I was when the war ended, whenever I stop to watch the stock quotations go by.

I don't have any feel for the market myself, Frank. I get my tips from the doorman, or the dentist. Sometimes I consult my horoscope in the hopes of learning something there, at least about how lucky I'm going to be that day.

One thing I do know is how lucky I am to have a pal like you, Frank, even if you do make me drink alone.

Come visit us.

Finkie

Dear Frank,

I don't have to believe it if I don't want to. I just read the letter you wrote to Aileen Mehle that ran in her column this morning, announcing your retirement from show business.

Aileen Mehle's an old friend of Odette's, Frank. She knew her for years before the Suzy column, when they were both actresses living in the same Hollywood boarding house, and so I got Aileen's phone number from Odette and called her as soon as I read your letter in the paper. But even as I was dialing "Suzy's" number, I started to feel a little foolish about calling. I thought to myself, Frank's fifty-five, he's reached the summit, why can't a guy go out on top?

But I have to admit, Frank, that night the arms of Morpheus were no comfort to me. I walked over to the river and looked out at Hoboken and the factories in the distance. You can't see Park Avenue (the Jersey one) from the river anymore, Frank, but I did see a steamship going up the Hudson, and I thought to myself—let him go—whatever this man has to do, let him go off and live on his mountain. We'll just have to get used to it, whatever is meant to happen to the weeping slobs like me, Frank, who felt every note as if it was coming out of their own throat—the slobs who never sleep, who pray for a day off, who love their daughters but hate their wives, who gamble around the clock until the clock runs out, and who finally get their picture in the paper, busted for killing their own compassion.

You're right, Francis, about what you said in your letter to "Suzy": it is the end of an era, our kind of show business is out of business. A lot of my friends are beginning to die off or can't get jobs. Five o'clock in the morning comes too early for me now, Frank.

I wouldn't be surprised if we walked down Fifth Avenue together if anyone under thirty would even give us a second look. Things have changed that much, Frank. I have to admit, Odette and I tried listening to *A Man Alone*, Frank, but I didn't understand what the poetry by Rod McKuen was supposed to mean.

I probably would've gone the rest of my life without reading a book, Frank, if it wasn't for all the waiting I had to do at the hospital when Odette was having her hysterectomy. Everyone knew better than to ask me to recommend a book, Frank, except for the kind of stuff I had to read in high school—you know, Shakespeare and stuff. But lately I've been looking through some of the first editions Odette had shipped to New York when she sold her house on North Roxbury Drive. I like James Thurber, for sure. I was always crazy about his cartoons but I never knew he was a writer. *The Old Man and the Sea* will make you cry, Frank. Odette even has a few of the books signed by the author. One of them is by a very prominent German writer who was living in Hollywood when Odette was in the picture business, Tom Mann. I've never been able to finish the book, but Odette says the signature will make the book even more valuable.

But I digress, Francis. When I listened to your voice on Watertown, I didn't know what to think. They had to carry me out of the cocktail lounge, Frank, when I heard you sing that John Denver song, "Rocky Mountain High."

When I took Odette to the opening night of *Dirty Dingus Magee*, Frank, there were only about ten other people in the theater and Odette thought the jokes were vulgar and so she went to sit in the lobby for the last half of the movie. I was just disappointed that you weren't in more of the scenes.

I know that Vice President Agnew thinks *Dirty Dingus Magee* is a great picture, Frank, but I'm sure he's a better politician than he is a movie critic even though, between you and me, Francis, I was a little jealous when I read that he'd been your guest in Palm Springs eighteen times this year.

I knew things were changing when I saw a copy of *A Man Alone* with a hole punched in the corner and about a hundred copies for sale in the Lexington Avenue drugstore on Sixty-sixth Street. They call it the Age of Aquarius, Frank. But I prefer to think of you walking briskly onto Rita Hayworth's yacht, wearing a crushable but never crushed hat with a narrow band, a tan colored topcoat slung over your shoulder regardless of the weather, and black calf shoes. I like to imagine us walking the streets of the city together, although I've read where you have to avoid most of the west fifties because you risk running into some old girlfriends who might want to reminisce, or an old captain from the Latin Quarter who might want to borrow some money. Those are the ones who never fail to recognize us as we walk down the street talking about our investments, or that weekend in Palm Springs when Ava showed up unexpectedly. We wind up at 21 where you know everyone's name. You tell me about a few of the waiters who you knew in the old roadhouse days, when you would come back from Hollywood and spend your money like it was going out of style. I notice how generous you are with the waiters and even the busboys, and not only when the meal is over, but in real life.

Your letter to "Suzy" said it was time to take a long pause and think. To try to understand the changes occurring in the world.

So go ahead, Frank, you shouldn't have to wait to do something like that. I told Odette that I doubted whether you ever had the chance to find out what you think about. Between being bossed around at work and jeered at by everybody else, most people probably never take the trouble to find out what they think.

So you may be stirring up a hornet's nest, Frank, but then again, it may be worth it.

But one thing I know for sure, Frank, when you give that farewell performance at the music center, Odette and I'll be there.

Your pal,

Finkie

Dear Frank,

Writing you this letter is the hardest thing I've ever done.

Before the night of June 14, 1971, I had spent over twenty years trying to come up with ways to meet you by accident. I gave a lot of thought to how we might run into each other. It seemed only reasonable that it would someday happen, perhaps at Jilly's or in the lobby of the Fountainbleu Hotel. The simplest plan was the best, to take a plane to Las Vegas and proceed by car to the Copa Room of the Sands. But for some reason, Frank, I never made that particular journey when you were in town. For the longest time I liked to think that it was simply a scheduling problem. After all, I had already seen Danny Thomas, Nat "King" Cole, and Sammy Davis at the Sands. I even remember when Sammy appeared as part of the "Will Mastin Trio Featuring Sammy Davis Jr." and I saw Floyd Paterson become champion of the world in Las Vegas, Frank. So it was always easy to say that you and I just passed each other like shipping clerks in the night.

But I think Odette is right, Frank. I think there's another reason. Odette says that I was missing you on purpose all those years. She says that if we actually met it would be harder to maintain the pretense that we had much in common.

But it's true, Frank, that right after planning some "accidental" meeting with you, I would abandon the idea and decide that I was needed in some other part of the country. The decent thing would have been to be honest with myself, that I was afraid to meet you, after all these years of keeping up a one-sided correspondence that very likely you were never even going to acknowledge.

I do think I might've seen you once, Frank. If it was you, you were in a car being driven by a man wearing a yellow sweater. You sat in the back smoking a cigarette. There were tired shadows under your eyes. The car was pulling away from the Lexington Avenue entrance of the Waldorf-Astoria Hotel. The next day there was a photograph of you in the *Journal-American*. The caption said that you had slipped into town to do some Christmas shopping. I was never sure if it was really you, Frank. Especially when later I read that an Italian film director whose trademark was beautiful yellow sweaters was also staying at the Waldorf.

But nothing in the world, Frank, would have kept Odette and I away from the music center that night. I was so nervous that entire day before the concert I thought I might not make it. I tried to imagine what it must be like for you, sitting in your dressing room, doodling on the list of songs. Maybe, like me, when you're nervous, you like to draw houses and cover up the windows and the front door with tiny lines as if no one lived there anymore. Maybe Don Rickles, I thought, will come into the room to cheer you up, to distract you from the job ahead. "You're gonna be great out there, Frank. People love pity, Frank." That guy kills me! I really hoped Rickles was nearby. I could've used him myself.

The thought of seeing you in person for the first time, the

last time, was more than my courage could bear, Francis. At one point I even told Odette she'd have to go to the music center without me. But she wouldn't hear of it. "You've waited a whole year for this moment, you've exhausted both of us just to get here. The time has come, Finkie," she said, "to face yourself."

Odette was right, Frank, but her words were still maddening to me. Didn't she know how badly I wanted to be there?

I knew how much care had gone into this night. I know you to be the most meticulous of men, you would have noticed that one empty seat, and I couldn't stand the fact that it would've been mine. And with Odette in her stunning pink gown. There'd be no end to my misery if I had done that to Odette, to you, to myself.

So I put on my tux and said a silent prayer. But my prayer was not answered. I didn't drop dead on the way to the music center.

Unfortunately, I don't remember very much about the concert itself, Frank. It seems to have passed by in a kind of blur. I do remember Roz Russell introducing you and you pointing your finger telling her not to cry.

I do remember when you first came out and we all stood up to welcome you. I remember when you started to sing "All or Nothing At All," and I whispered to Odette, "For god's sake, he's going all the way back, back to the thirties and Harry James, back to "Nancy with the Laughing Face)," and "I've Got You Under My Skin," and in no time at all, Jill and Nancy Ava and Rosalie were in the room with us, and I had no quarrel with the past. I just listened, helpless, as you dropped the net of my life over me. I remember when you sang "Fly Me to the Moon," and I started banking a little to the left like Rosalie and I used to do on those airplane trips.

I remember what you said about how you built your career on singing saloon songs, and how gently you started "Angel Eyes," then stopped to light a cigarette. Wreathed in smoke, you reached the last line of the song, "Excuse me while I disappear." And then you did. Odette noticed Cary Grant, crying by now, and Gregory Peck removing his aviator glasses and putting a handkerchief up to his face. And I saw David Frost looking vanquished in the dress circle, too weak to take the microphone from you and thank everyone for coming. I saw Roz Russell embrace you in the wings. And that's where I start to be unable to think properly, Frank. Unable to explain to all these visitors I've had lately what exactly happened to yours truly.

I do know that for a minute or two after the house lights came on Odette leaned over with a sad little smile on her face and kissed me. I knew that in a few moments this part of my life would be over. I knew that I would spend a lot of time sitting out on the balcony in the warm sun, thinking about this night, thinking about Sinatraland. I knew I'd have to remind myself repeatedly in the days and weeks ahead that nothing lasts forever. I felt at various times in my life, Frank, that in Sinatraland we lived in a kind of dream, a dream in which nothing was real but the waiting, whether it was waiting for night to come or waiting for the women for whom we cause so much pain.

But it's impossible to thrive in that world, Frank—just waiting, so I told Odette that I was going backstage to thank you and say goodbye. For about ten seconds Odette tried to hold me back, grabbing me by the wrist and telling me how many people would be backstage at a time like this. She looked frightened for me, Frank.

But I told Odette that tonight was the perfect night to introduce myself and talk about the old neighborhood in Hoboken. That this might be the only chance I'd ever have to understand you a little better, to make it easier to say goodbye.

It was strange, Frank, but there weren't nearly as many people backstage as I imagined. The first person I recognized was Nancy Jr. It looked like she was having an argument with Robert Wagner over whose car to take to Rosalind Russell's house for the big party. I heard people laughing and a few champagne corks being popped.

Then a shadow came over me, Frank. This shadow had a walkie-talkie and was blocking my way. Then another shadow appeared with a gun in his hand. The two shadows started talking. "You didn't let this fellow get inside, did you?" The other shadow seemed to ignore the question. "What the fuck are you doing here, you son of a bitch?" the shadow with the walkie-talkie asked me. "Trying to get in to see Frank," I said. "Have you been talking to this man?" the shadow with the gun in his hand asked the other shadow, the one with the walkie-talkie. "No," answered the shadow with the walkie-talkie. "Shut-up," the gun-holding shadow said to him. "I'm interrogating this prisoner." "Who is this hebe shithead?" asked a third shadow who completed a circle around me. "He's a goddamm reporter," one of the shadows said. "You're a goddamn son-of-a-bitch," said the newest shadow, "You son-of-a-bitch motherfucker. You kike." I think by now there were at least five shadows standing over me, Frank. One of them went at me with both fists, driving into my belly. One punch would've been enough, Frank. But they kept coming. I heard one of them say that I had to be taught a lesson for sticking my big nose in where it didn't belong and why did I have to go and spoil Frank's beautiful evening?

I think that's when my head got split open. A guy they called Banjo came at me with a blackjack three feet long. I think I broke his nose before I passed out. I knew I was really going to get it, Frank, when one of the shadows took off his jacket and held it up as a shield so that no one but the other shadows could see what they were doing to me. I heard Odette screaming in the hallway, Frank. It broke my heart to hear her crying out "Why did you do that to him? He loves you!"

Even then, one of the shadows wasn't quite finished with me, Frank. He came at me like a pile driver with both hands. Later, I was able to identify him because everytime he hit me I had a close-up view of this huge diamond ring that kept gouging me in the left eyebrow. Believe it or not, Frank, I managed to get as far as the fire exit when I got hit on the back of the head.

I don't know which of the shadows hit me, but I do know he was wearing a gray silk suit. I know this because I saw my blood all over it. I was happy about that, Frank. I thought at least he'll never be able to wear that suit again.

That's when I checked out for good and woke up in the hospital, with my head bandaged like the Invisible Man and multiple fractures in my legs. But at least the shadows were gone. For a while I saw them in my sleep, or imagined them standing over my bed.

I have a hard time being understood by the nurses, Frank. First, because my lip is split and second, because the doctors say that I took some real punishment to my head and that'll take a few weeks for the accident, you might call it, to run its course. That's when I'll be able to speak more clearly. It's actually easier to write. That's why I haven't been able to return your phone calls, Frank.

Although, I want you to know that I don't hold you responsible for what happened to me.

For years people have said to me, "Finkie, aren't you tired of this one-sided conversation with Frankie? Don't you ever want to say, "Fuck you, Frank. I'm not going to put up with your bullshit, anymore?" But I don't feel that way, Francis, and I never have. I know you wouldn't have had this happen for the world. But what can you do when a grenade goes off like that? I remember from the war those Mills grenades, how when they went off those little squares go off in twenty directions. It was like that night, Frank. One of the guys tries to be a big man, the hero of the hour, and before long people are fighting, drawing guns and swearing to kill each other.

Odette is a different story, Frank. She's not going to be so easy to convince. She says something like this was inevitable with so many people around you. Odette told Nancy Ava, who flew in yesterday, that she believes that what happened to me after the show was the result of years of telling dirty stories, breaking furniture, tearing up hotel rooms, pinching waitresses, and betting on the horses. She said that even if you don't order someone to be beaten up, you allow it to happen, as Odette puts it, "by keeping the company you keep."

The doctors came by to see me today, Frank. One of them said that he hadn't seen a guy that bad off since the army. The head of security for the music center called today, too, Frank. He said there wasn't anything on the police blotter about the incident, but that he just wanted me to know that as soon as he heard about the commotion backstage he went back there and started pulling guys off me.

I heard that you refused to be interviewed about what happened, but "Suzy" told Odette that you felt terrible about what happened and that you've even offered to pay my hospital bills. I remember once, a long time ago, Frank, I teased you about paying some of my medical expenses. I certainly never thought all these years later that you would have reason to take it seriously.

I'm starting to hear from people I only used to dream about meeting. Dean sent me a bouquet of roses that was so big it couldn't fit in the room, Frank. Angie Dickinson—Angie Dickinson!—sent me a stuffed tiger, along with a note that said,

"To Finkie, hope you're on the prowl again soon. Love, Angie." Had I known I was going to get all of this attention, Frank, I would've gotten myself beat up by your bodyguards long before your retirement.

But in all seriousness, Frank, I know how badly you must feel. I want to thank you for all the food you sent, too. Unfortunately, I can't chew very much now. It's awful having all this wonderful food and not being able to eat any of it. The guy in the next room keeps coming into my room and stealing the food. I finally caught him at it and told him that if he wasn't getting enough to eat, he should complain to the nurse or his doctor. He came up and whispered in my ear that the hospital food wasn't enough, and that even though he tried, he wasn't able to make doo-doo. He said that he saw them bringing in all this food and thought that it might help him.

I can't wait to get out of the hospital, Frank. Even though my mouth is still swollen (even my tongue hurts), I could really use a drink. I know it would help me to sleep and help get me to that point where I might have a better view of what happened.

Odette thinks that what happened to me should be the last straw. But you can't make a guy lie to himself, Frank. It's true, I dug a grave for you while I lay here in the dark covered in bandages and hanging from wires. But the more I learn about what happened that night, and the more I hear about how you haven't been able to sleep or eat the last couple of days, the more I want to say, that for the first time, Frank, I'm glad I'm not you. I wouldn't want to feel the way you must feel right now.

I never considered myself a very smart guy, Frank. But I can tell from the hat and raincoat on the hat rack in my room that you've probably been to visit me in the hospital sometime in the past few days. You might even be here right now for all I know.

Get one of the boys to drive you home. I don't feel much like talking. Or anything else. Right now, Frank, it feels as if the world was made for sleeping.

Fink

EVERYTHING HAPPENS TO ME

Dear Jill,

So where the hell is Petoskey, Michigan? Nancy Ava said you and your new husband will be moving there in the fall. She said I shouldn't be worried about you because you and your husband are coining money in Philly and you've even got a servant living in the house.

I can't tell you how much it meant to me to see you, Jill, while I was laid up after the altercation at the music center. At first I was afraid you were going to give me one of your lectures about how I was living an "overextended youth," and that this is what happens when you refuse to accept the unhappy frustrations of middle age.

But you surprised me by showing nothing but kindness and loyalty to me during that difficult time. For some time after the "accident," it seemed as if the only people I saw were doctors and people who were offering legal advice. I even got a call from Melvin Belli, in San Francisco (he was Jack Ruby's lawyer), offering to help me if I would press charges against Frank and his bodyguards. He told me that he had heard of other cases similar to mine, though not as serious, and that he thought it was time "someone put a stop to Sinatra's bullying ways."

He even mentioned Frederick Weisman and the Beverly Hills Polo Lounge. I told Mr. Belli that while I appreciated his interest, I had no intention of filing a lawsuit against Mr. Sinatra, and I told him that I was getting a lot of those kinds of calls, usually from lawyers, urging me to go after Frank because he has money, and that the only way to punish someone like that is through his pocketbook.

I had tears in my eyes when I told him that I had spent my life listening to Frank Sinatra—that he had been with me when I went from being a boy to a man. That he made me feel potent. That he had been with me when I was a young salesman passing through towns and cities with the radio on. That his voice was my consolation prize when our marriage ended, and that whenever I thought of Rosalie, which was usually whenever I thought about how much effort goes into being alive, that's when I hear his voice and imagine him putting on his raincoat and stepping out with me into the unknown future.

I don't know if I was making any sense at that point, but it was certainly the truth, and I guess how I felt about all this must have gotten back to Frank, because it wasn't too long after that, that I got a phone call in New York from Frank himself, offering me a job with his "dago secret service," as he called it.

"You'll be the only Yid in the detail, Finkie," Frank said, "You'll keep 'em honest." Then he told me that he was going to put Jilly on the phone, and that "Mr. Rizzo will give you all the details," and that he hoped to see me in Palm Springs by the end of the week.

I told Jilly that I was honored that Frank would consider me for his security detail, but that I couldn't figure out why some of the guys who four months ago nearly beat me to death would want to work with me now. Jilly said that Frank had removed some of the "pimps" who had exploited their position with him to hurt guys, and that Frank believed that only someone who had been seriously hurt by security guards would know the difference between a real threat and someone who wanted an autograph.

Then he put Frank back on, and Frank told me to discuss it with Odette and get back to him in a few days. When he gave me his private number, my hand was shaking so badly I almost couldn't read it.

There are times in a man's life when it seems that all he ever does is watch women cry. Odette must've felt that way, Jill, in the days following Frank's call. Just at the point when I was wondering what I was going to do with my life, they decide to re-open Sinatraland.

Odette asked me why Frank would need another security man if he had decided to retire. But the truth is, Frank retired for about five minutes. Jilly said that he knew Frank was going to get back in the ring when he went into the hospital for a new set of hair plugs. In fact, one of my first duties was going to be nursing Frank through his second hair transplant. The guys thought this was a good idea, being that I had just spent so much time in the hospital that I was practically a doctor myself.

You can imagine, Jill, what Odette thought of the whole thing.

She said that for the first time in our marriage, the light changed from green to yellow. She said that at her age, she wasn't interested in waiting weeks for me to come home. She said she didn't want to have to worry if Frank was going to make me eat eggs and bacon off a hooker's stomach, which in the old days, I once heard, used to be part of the initiation ceremony for Frank's bodyguards.

But I would never do anything to hurt Odette, Jill, and the thought of losing her would have been enough reason for me to turn the job down cold. After all this time, I still worry that I'm not a good enough husband and I'm always telling people that Odette got the short end of the stick when it comes to our marriage.

But Frank made it hard to turn him down. He offered to set up one of the cottages next to the main house for Odette and me. Telling us that when he travels it's usually only to L.A. or Vegas; another staff takes care of his overseas visits and that even those happen less often now because he is trying to slow down and spend more time with the family. He says he's becoming more involved in politics, especially since Ronnie Reagan became governor and that's another reason for him to stay close to home. Frank says that he's trying to convince his friend, Vice President Agnew, to run for the presidency.

As Nancy Ava probably told you by now, Odette and I

moved to Palm Springs in time to spend Christmas with Frank, Nancy Jr. and her husband Hugh Lambert, Frank's youngest daughter Tina, Frank's mother Dolly (who remembered my parents but didn't understand how Myron and I figured into the equation—Dolly said she thought she had performed an abortion on my mother and didn't realize she had had any children after that), and Frank's first ex-wife, who they call Big Nancy. She spent the entire holiday sinking into the sofa and watching television. Occasionally she would reach out and touch Frank's hand, and ask him how he spent his day, but he usually pulls away and she just becomes quiet again.

My first trip with Frank and the guys was to Caesar's Palace, where Frank was going to start his "comeback." There were thirteen hundred people packed into the Circus Maximus showroom, Jill, and everyone was given a gold coin inscribed, "Hail Sinatra, The Noblest Roman Has Returned," and it was marked with the date: January 25, 1974.

It was Frank's first time in front of a live audience since that fateful night two and a half years before.

I can't describe to you Jill, what it's like to sit up all night drinking Stoli, listening to him talk about the old days and what it was like to be in the White House with Lyndon Johnson, the two men getting massages in the middle of the night, and him wondering, "Was it possible after all that there was no such thing as love?"

You were right about one thing, though. Frank does have a temper. I've seen him blow up at one of the boys down here and

I assure you it's not a pretty sight. Take what happened to Andy Celentano. I guess of all the guys here I'm closest to Andy. He's a rich kid, Jill, whose whole family has been crazy about Frank since the beginning. Like me, I guess. Andy's grandparents started a frozen food business using recipes from the old country. Frank loves the pizza pies and so we stock a walk-in freezer with hundreds of them.

But Andy was never interested in the family business, he just wanted to be in Frank's presence all the time—Andy says to watch Frank walk through a door is a thing of beauty. But occasionally Frank will lose his temper, even at a sweet kid like Andy Celentano. Once Andy made some remark about all these books that were starting to come out about President Kennedy and his womanizing, he said something to the effect that where there's smoke there's got to be fire, or something pretty innocent like that—Frank just exploded. He said that Andy was just an ignorant wop kid and didn't a know a thing about Jack Kennedy. Then around five o clock in the morning, Frank let himself into Andy's room and took all the beautiful clothes Frank had bought for him and cut them up with a scissors and threw all the torn up clothes into the pool. The next day Frank apologized to Andy and went with him into town to buy an entire new wardrobe.

Frank is a complex guy, Jill. There's no getting away from it.

I'm not sure I even understand his sense of humor. For example, a few weeks ago Frank was at the Bing Crosby Golf Tournament here in Palm Springs. I was Frank's caddie, which was a tremendous thrill for me, as you can well imagine. Frank, though, was not in a good mood. He was off his game, and between you and me and the lamppost, Frank never really forgave Bing Crosby for "stealing" President Kennedy away from him.

So Frank gets himself into a sand trap, I could tell that he wanted to blow off some steam but the whole event is on live television, so what can he do?

So he says to me, "Finkie? What time is it? Do you have the time, Fink?" While I'm looking at my watch, Frank grabs my wrist and tears the Rolex off my arm, looks at it and throws it into the sand trap.

Frank had given me that watch when I first got to Palm Springs. It was by that watch, Jill, that I counted the hours, weeks, and months I was in Frank's service, and now he had me sifting through a ton of sand to find it.

Like I said, a complicated guy.

Frank once told us that he was thinking of writing a book. He even kept a couple of notebooks by his bed. And for a while there, he really seemed to be filling them up with "the story"— as it came to be known around here.

Frank liked telling us "the story" and embellishing it each time. The hero was a guy who lived in the desert but can see everything there is to see in the world. He is given a certain gift, in this case, an astonishing voice. This voice gives him tremendous power. But the problem comes when the man who possesses this instrument cannot decide how to make use of it.

Whether or not to use his talent for good or ill. At that moment he is transported to the place where he began his journey, a place filled with streetcars and churches, and old ladies leaning out of windows, and he walks along these streets, though he is invisible to all. And he walks past a building which is very familiar to him, but he can't quite remember why. Once inside, he moves through the different rooms of the house, a place which is strangely comforting to him. Eventually, he realizes that this was once *his* house, and that everyone who lived there is dead. At the very top of the house, he discovers a man inhabiting the darkest room. This man tells him that only by using his gift of a beautiful voice will the house again be filled with the living. And so he devotes himself to this, working to the utmost limit of his talents. But when he returns to the house of his beginnings, expecting to find it bustling with life, it is emptier and darker than ever. This turns him into a man no longer respectful of his gifts but someone whose experience of the world has left him as cold and dark and empty as that house.

Odette, who's become a voracious reader out here in the desert, says that the hero in Frank's story is really Frank. If that's true, I'm not the one who knows.

It may surprise you to hear this, Jill, after all we've been through, but I've never stopped loving you. I've never even entertained the idea of pretending not to love you. I know we will always have Nancy Ava. She's partly the reason for having good relations with each other, but I'm sure that's not the only reason. I just wanted you to know that you're probably what the magazine writers would call my big love.

I'm writing to you, Jill, because I don't want you to feel sorry for me. You used to say how sorry you felt for me, but I'm sure you meant that back in the days when I wasn't listening, when it seemed as if I was the last person on earth who would undergo some kind of change. But I have, Jill, as you can tell. I don't know exactly how it happened or when, but I know that it's true.

I don't even get angry anymore about that terrible night at the back of the music center. For I know that some of the shadows who surrounded me are probably some of the same men who live in this house with me now.

Odette says she can't fathom how I can work with men who I know once tried to kill me. But I told her that what these men did that night was the result of their love for Frank. That everyone loves in their own way. Perhaps they were being unfaithful to that love, but that's how it started out. I can see that now, when I walk through a hotel lobby with a walkie-talkie in my hand, clearing a path so that a moody man who knows everyone's dreams can walk through the night.

I started this letter for one reason and one reason only, to tell you not to worry about me. I've always wanted to move to the desert and here I am. You can see the San Jacinto Mountains from Frank's living room. This is where Frank says he wants to spend his time, painting and reading history. (Wouldn't you know, that's my luck, to hook up with Frank Sinatra just when he wants to turn himself into an egghead.)

Well, I can't say I blame him. Odette says that maybe Frank

knows other men's grief better than his own. She likes to say that on Frank's face you can see the fate of every human desire, except love. Which is kind of funny, when you think about how Frank's voice drifting over from the hi-fi always gave a guy courage to caress the woman he loved. So I always thought Odette's comment was a little harsh. No one knows how to love, Jill, we just do the best we can.

Your ex and future pal,

Finkie

P.S. We did have a lot of fun together, didn't we?

Dear Frank,

This is one letter I know you're not going to answer. Frank, how could you leave us here, you goddamn son-of-a-bitch? I'm still getting over the death of the long playing record and now this had to happen.

Odette's therapist thinks this could be the most important letter I've ever written you—because now I really have to let you go. But what she doesn't know, Frank, is that I did that a long time ago. I thought, that after Jill's death, after all the time Nancy Ava and I spent in that room looking at those manicured nails on that bony hand, that nothing else would be able to reach in and kill me like that again. But I was wrong. I didn't figure on this.

I think I should tell you how it happened. Odette and I had gotten in the habit of going every year to Elie Wiesel's lectures at the 92nd Street Y. Ever since I read that Michael Milken was studying the Torah, I thought it was something I should take a little more seriously. So Odette bought us season tickets to Wiesel's lectures. (It had been a long time since that disastrous day—when I had my bar mitzvah. On that day, one of my uncles came by the house and dragged me off to temple. My father was already dead and no one else from our family even came to the service. The congregation, which consisted of about twenty surly men, forced me to stumble over some passages in the Bible which they pointed to with a silver-plated pointer shaped like a finger. It scared the shit out of me. When we got home, some of the grown-ups were already sharing a bottle of schnaaps and talking about the unbearable noise in the laundry business my father had left these bums. I sat on the couch waiting for my present, a new watch, but it never came. A few years later, after my mother died, I searched through her things looking for the watch. I was convinced that she had withheld it because she had heard, probably from my uncle, about how poorly I read the Hebrew words. There, in one of her drawers, I found my watch, out of date, but mine. Every appointment I've ever missed, I've missed by that watch, Frank.)

I've gotten way off course, Frank, but my mind is racing and I'm not quite certain why I'm even doing this, but maybe it'll help somehow. I was about to tell you how it happened. After Wiesel's lecture, I took Odette for a drink across the street into a real workingman's bar on Lexington Avenue, and that's where we heard the news. Odette said I practically bellowed and tried to reach for her but that I looked like a man who had just been scalded by a pot of coffee and this was the moment before he would begin to scream. But I didn't scream, Frank, in fact, I don't remember saying anything at all. I just left the bar and started walking. I must've walked all over the city. Later, Odette told me, she was following me all night in a cab.

Whoever said that after the first death, the rest are easier to take, didn't have to work for a living, Frank. I didn't figure on this. The same roaring in the ears, the pounding in my chest. At my age, Frank, every death is a stage whisper, loud enough for everyone to hear. I'm not a poet, Frank, and I don't want to sound like some Hamburger Hamlet (I saw Peter Lawford there once. He lived up the hill from the Hamburger Hamlet on Sunset. He looked like hell, smoking a cigarette in one of those purple booths—emaciated, ashamed that someone had recognized him, poor Peter, King of the Pimps) but in a strange way, once the shock wore off, I started to get mad. I hated hearing all that crap about how you "went out your way," and what a beautiful man you were to all your friends, and how it's really the end of an era. Because, as I told Odette, "The truth is, Frank's death finally caught up with him." I remember one night, when we were out for dinner and a very pretty young girl giggling with delight came up to ask you for your autograph and you, Frank, weary as I ever saw you, signed the menu with a look in your eyes that I never forgot. It was a look that went from wanting to cry to one that looked as if you wanted to kill. At that moment, you seemed like a man who wanted to empty out his life of everything. The past as well as the future. It was the look of a man who had spent too much time in the company of the kind of men he had known when he was young. It was almost as though, after an endless and empty journey, you had come home to find that no one recognized you; you had become a stranger.

I'm not saying, Frank, that you might have welcomed death, but that what was "grown up" and "thrilling" about your life had been over for a very long time. For what is a swinger or hipster, anyway, but someone who loves the pleasures of the world more than the world itself, who loves the world more than himself? I don't know if I ever told you how frustrating it was for me to go to work for you just about the time you decided to become a fucking philosopher, and think about life while working on your electric railroad trains in that special room no one was allowed to enter. I worked so hard studying every movement and gesture I ever saw you make. I could light a cigarette not only like you, but better than you, and then you go off to your house in the desert and give it up.

Nancy Ava reminded me that I was there when you collapsed onstage in Richmond, Virginia. (Nancy Ava remembered because she was with us on that tour. She and I hadn't been that far south since she was a little girl. I had taken her to Washington when I was called to testify before the Kefauver Crime Commission, to explain those envelopes stuffed with cash Jill's father asked me to hold for him when he went into the hospital for his operation—how could I have known half of 47th

Street was paying him for hot coats? Although, his keeping me in the dark about everything finally paid a dividend.) It was on that tour I began to notice that words on the TelePrompTer getting bigger and bigger until the words for "I Got You under My Skin" started to look like the print in those *Weekly Readers* Nancy Ava used to bring home from school. I knew we wouldn't be on the road much longer.

I guess the thing that really upset me the most was the way you treated Frankie Jr. The kid's a good singer, and he looks and sounds a lot like you know who. I don't know whose idea it was to give him that name, but it stunk. It was a rotten thing to do. It was like naming your kid "Fuck You, Junior." But the worst was when you invited him to become your music director. I know how much he loved traveling all over the world with you, but the way you treated him onstage was unbelievable to me! Back home no one believed me when I told them how you would humiliate the kid in front of thousands of people; making faces at him behind his back. It broke my fucking heart to see the idol of my youth so angry about getting old that he would take it out on a younger man who looked like him and sounded like him in the days when he was King of the World and spitting in its eye. You couldn't stand that, and so you'd put Frankie down. I remember thinking to myself, "It must make him feel better to do that, the poor bastard."

I'm sure in a funny way, Frankie Jr. must be feeling worse than anyone right now. Because in some weird way he must feel free of you, free of having to live in that shadow, free of having to turn his back on the audience while you got the chance to make love to it. Free of having to go backstage and pump some life into the old man, giving him all of his juice, having to pour what's left of his own life into Frank's, for one last show. I don't think you have to be Sigmund Freud or even smoke a pipe to figure it out, that if Frank Sinatra Jr. feels a little bit freer tonight, then he must be feeling guilty as hell for feeling that way. If I saw him right now, I would say, "Don't worry, Frankie. Your father loved you, he just played the tough guy for so long he didn't know how to show it. And anyway, we dump all our disappointments on our kids. Conceived out of joy, they are also conceived with the most tremendous ignorance of the future, and so at the end, we give them grief for all the fears we weren't able to conquer." That's what I would tell Frank Jr. about his old man. That, and get back on the road. But do your own songs, don't turn yourself into a human yarzheit candle for Frank Sinatra.

I know you would've been interested, Francis, to learn that *Unsolved Mysteries* approached me about appearing on their show, but that I refused. You would've been proud of me turning down all that publicity, but I just couldn't go through all that again, the endless questions and looking through mugshots.

I used to think that show was really a form of grave robbing, I had no idea it could do so much good. The man they described in a hat with a speech impediment who asked to use the bathroom near the Haines's boathouse sounded a lot like the groundskeeper for the private golf course Geoffrey had built near his house. I don't know how they dug that up. But it looks after all this time that it wasn't Geoffrey Haines who had murdered Rosalie, but this pathetic guy who thought Rosalie was interested in him because she had taken some ice tea out to him from time to time. I guess even bad television can be a force for good in the world. It's sad, though, that Geoffrey Haines had to live the rest of his life under a cloud like that.

I wanted more than anything to prolong the kind of life I had with you and the boys. What others called sin, we thought of as fun and probably still do. But it was my own fear that cast me out of Sinatraland. The fear that my family, Nancy Ava mostly, might shut me out because my life was in such a perpetual state of disorder that seemed so natural to me. It was simply my life.

But I have lived in Sinatraland a long time. My first wife is buried there, along with the past, and now you, Frank. I gave up a lot to live in Sinatraland. Nancy Ava hated you. She felt it was you, Francis, who robbed her of the chance to have her mother and father together. But I've often told her that that wasn't Frank Sinatra's fault, he was responsible for his own life—and only his own life. I have to accept the blame for all that living in Sinatraland has brought down on the house of Finkelstein, the way that an oyster has to accept the blame for the pearl. It's time I stopped writing this letter, Frank. The world is filling up with the dead and I can only think of how much time I've already wasted.

P.S. If you screw Jill up there I'll never talk to you again.